ASHLIGHT

GUARDIANS OF SATERA BOOK ONE

by

BREANNA PETSCH

Published by Mystic Grove Media LLC. Washington, United States of America.

ISBN 979-8-218-78520-8

Cover design and Interior formatting: White Rose Publishing by "Sienna Arts"

First Edition 2025

For every dreamer who chooses hope over letting the ashes settle.

- B.P.

Contents

Chapter 1

Aiella's heart pounded as she sat up in the icy darkness, dragging her legs over the side of her cot as her face found her hands. *One, two, three.* She inhaled, holding her breath to steady her trembling body. She had dreamed the same nightmare again, this time more haunting and vivid than ever.

"Ella?" She heard a whisper across the black den, squinting through her fingers. A large figure was slowly making its way through the rows of normal people who were still slumbering. "Ella? Are you okay?" Frank asked again, taking a quiet seat beside her on the bed. She tiredly shook her head, leaning against his shoulder.

"Come," he said, his shadow offering a hand. "We will talk while we eat."

The sleeping chamber was not large, but walking across it on tiptoe while everyone was still enjoying their dreams always lent itself to be an interesting challenge. Last week, she tripped while trying to find her way through the maze of bodies, holding in a yelp while somehow falling directly onto Eli of all people. She felt herself flushing at the memory, holding her breath to be extra cautious as she snuck by him this time.

"You all right?" Eli mumbled near-inaudibly as she passed.

"Yes," she whispered back. That warm, familiar feeling grew in the pit of her stomach. For a second, she even forgot how empty it felt. Eli said nothing as Aiella heard him roll over in his cot. He was still asleep. She breathed a sigh of relief, her gut letting out a slow growl.

Ducking her head ever so slightly to exit the sleep chambers, she moved the curtains aside, placing them back in position as quickly as possible to stop the sudden brightness from waking anyone. It smelled damper than usual today. The snow and ice must have finally melted up ahead, as they had hoped. Shivers ran down her spine as she wrapped her arms around herself.

"Your cheeks are looking a little red, Ella," Frank said with a chuckle. She turned defensively, but her body betrayed her with a nervous laugh. A huge grin plastered itself on him as he grabbed two of the last remaining dried fish pieces for them to nibble on.

"Why are you always so persistent about the two of us?" Aiella asked, sucking the salt off and savoring it as she sat opposite him at the dusty counter. She looked around mindlessly, wondering if she would ever grow used to this world, lit only by candlelight and haphazard battery-powered lamps, which reminded her that the batteries for those and the small griddle would need to be charged soon. She tapped her foot against the broken barstool impatiently as she remembered she was finally going back to the surface again today. A smile spread across her face; her nightmare forgotten. *They would not starve.*

"Ah, see!" Frank said, clapping his hands together. "The thought of you two together makes you happy, too!" Aiella rolled her eyes, though she still smiled.

"I am too busy helping you to have any sort of romantic relationship," she retorted. *Not that she had helped much this last time.* Frank may not be her biological father, but he was as close a thing to a dad as she would ever get. "Besides," she added, "It isn't like—"

"Okay, okay," Frank cut her off, raising his hands. "I'll back off. Just remember, our happiness is one of the few things we are in control of, my dear girl. Alta and I are happy together, even though I still miss my family every single day."

While he went shuffling through the old cupboards, crafted years before out of a blend of scrap material, Aiella bit her lip, disagreeing. The world around them was underwhelming. How was anyone supposed to be happy living underground their entire life after losing everything? She arrived at the tunnels when they were still being finished, although she couldn't remember much from then since she was only a few years old. Eli arrived a couple of years after that, a young boy who was filthy and short-tempered.

He had been on his own, or at least not remembering anyone else, for a year, somehow surviving in the dark world that the country had become. Like many of them, he lost his parents. It had been ten times as many allies to start, crammed together in this den that housed them. Aiella couldn't recall much from those years, but she did faintly remember how close together everyone seemed.

Everyone thought that their location in the forested mountains would save them from the fantastical contagion wiping out the country and the world, but it eventually found them. It cut their numbers in half at first, sweeping across anyone who had been out in the wilderness and the nearby bigger city. With everyone having such close contact... There were just fourteen of them left now, with her, Eli, Luke, and Alexis being the only ones who weren't at least middle-aged. It had been just them for years and years. Having space to isolate was a privilege they didn't have, so here they all stayed, no one ever leaving. It wasn't worth the risk.

"You had the same nightmare again, didn't you?" Frank asked her, interrupting her thoughts. She nodded.

"I could have gotten everyone killed if this storm didn't pass," she said. Everyone here agreed a long time ago that they would not leave the safety net of their underground home again, not after the losses they had all suffered. People could walk out of the living area to the corridor that slanted towards freedom—the slits of ventilation straight through the cliff side stone allowing for much fresher air there—but they all decided long ago not to climb out. They wouldn't expose themselves, not to anyone or anything. The latter being most prevalent. Only Aiella went hunting to limit overall risk, a sacrifice she was proud to make.

After an encounter with the mountain lion a few weeks ago, though, a freak blizzard kept them all huddled together, hoping for a miracle as their food stock vanished far too quickly. Aiella didn't have the means to dress appropriately in that kind of weather, so the freak winter storm meant she wasn't able to return to the surface only a few days later, like she had planned. Unfortunately, the number of provisions was lacking in preparedness, even by their standards.

"Is it still starvation in the dream, mostly?" He questioned.

"Yes," she replied, "Though there was also a strange beam of light shooting up into space this time, and fire..." When she said it out loud, there was no real reason for her to become so shaken up by it. Down here, they were safe from the fiery affliction that had destroyed the lives of so many. Since she left to hunt and gather every fortnight, it convinced her that the surrounding region was safe as well.

Frank shrugged. "It is just a dream, dear girl." But his face darkened as he let out a sigh and frowned, counting out the last of their current rations quietly before setting them down in front of her. "A cougar stalked you, Ella. You lost what you had hunted for the day. It wasn't in your control that a storm hit." *But I chose not to hunt for more;* her thoughts silently screamed. The distinction was weighing heavily on her. Frank continued, "I worry about it, too, you know. Lack of resources. Of sunshine. But you're going to go out again, and we're all going to be okay! All right? I know it's a stressful life. It's not normal for humans to live underground. I just don't see what any of us could do. The world is still such—"

"A dangerous place," Aiella finished for him. "I know." A small spider caught her attention at the curved corner of the room, making its way along the thick dirt walls, almost blending in.

Straining her eyes to see, she set her chin on her hand. Her blinks became longer and longer, her body finally giving in to its exhaustion while her mind fought against it. Her focus went black.

"Hey!" A voice shouted from across the way, startling her awake. She looked to her right just in time to see it was Luke coming through the curtain before she promptly lost her balance on the stool and toppled over.

"Ella!" Alexis exclaimed, giggling as she rushed into the small kitchen behind Luke. Aiella grinned. She always loved when these two were together, which was often given their living space. Paired with Frank, they were the closest thing to a family she could hope for.

"There was a spider," Aiella told them slowly, reaching one hand to her head. "Ouch, I must have fallen asleep." She burst out into a much-needed fit of laughter with them. Her backside was aching from landing on the hard, earthy floor, but at least no one else besides Alexis and Luke saw.

"I'll say," Eli said, making his presence on the left side of the room known as he walked over to reach out a hand. Aiella froze, heat filling her face. Alexis widened her eyes at her, biting back even more laughter while Luke didn't even try to stop. Aiella slowly turned her head, tipping her head to the side as she peered up at the lumbering young man before her. *Why are you blushing?* She scolded herself.

"So, you're watching me sleep now, are you?" Aiella asked, cocking her head even more.

"You wish," he returned, smiling that familiar sideways grin. She could feel Alexis' and Luke's giddy stares on the back of her head.

"I definitely don't." Yet she smiled up at him.

"Are you going to grab his hand, or what?" Luke finally asked. Alexis broke into another frenzy of giggles, covering her face as Aiella glared at her from the corner of her eye.

"It's a valid question," Eli admitted, his arm still extended. Rolling her eyes, Aiella grabbed his smooth hand, his strength taking her by surprise as he pulled her up. Her hair was in disarray, covering half of her face.

"Are you okay?" He asked softly, his fingers gently tucking her stray hairs behind her ear.

"I'm fine," she replied. "They just surprised me. Next time I'm sleeping, give me a warning before you yell, will you?" She looked over at Luke, crossing her arms and holding back a smile.

"I didn't know you were sleeping!" He objected. Aiella felt Eli's hand tenderly touch her shoulder, his presence then slipping out of the curtain towards the main living room. She breathed a silent sigh, her chest unwinding.

"Sure, and what about all the others still asleep?" Aiella prodded Luke.

"We were the last up," he said matter-of-factly. Aiella raised an eyebrow.

"I was telling Luke we should bug you to show us the outdoor world," Alexis told her, nudging him playfully while a faint blush formed on his cheeks. Aiella looked back and forth at them both, amused by their painstakingly obvious feelings they tried to act oblivious to.

Luke took a deep breath, relaxing. "Well, Ai? Do you think you could? Please?"

Aiella sighed, knowing they would not like her answer. "You know I can't," she said sadly.

"But why not?" Alexis pressed. "There hasn't been an outbreak here in years, right?"

Aiella shook her head, her hands falling from her chest and finding her baggy pockets instead. How old were these pants at this point? She couldn't remember who had passed them down to her. There were scarce resources they all had to split, items such as clothing included. She looked up at where the spider was on the wall earlier, long gone now. Squinting, she could see a cobweb forming in a crevice in the shadows of the cavern ceiling. She would need to remember to grab a branch to clear it off later.

"It is too risky. You guys are like my little siblings. I could never put you in danger like that." She so badly wanted to wipe away the immediate frowns that met her. It *was* too risky, though, right? Frank was especially firm on that. The wildlife alone was a problem. "Besides, I have to go out for food today."

Luke and Alexis nodded their heads slowly. "You'll be able to get enough for the next few weeks this time? In case another storm hits?" Luke asked with wide eyes.

"Yes," Aiella assured them, both exhaling loudly. Their youthful faces looked more gaunt than usual, the lack of nutrients clear. "You said everyone is awake?"

"Mmhm," Alexis answered, crisscrossing her arms to point fingers at both the archway behind Aiella and the one on the opposite side of the room. Just as she finished speaking, Alta immediately barged through the curtain of the sleeping quarters.

"Ella! Come quickly. The Elder is acting strangely and asking for you."

"Really?" Aiella asked. The Elder rarely spoke to anyone, let alone her. Curious, she followed Alta through the crinkled curtains. Dust hung in the air as a permanent side effect of having dirt walls as she stepped through the next compacted archway across the room. She needed to remember to help Frank wipe the counter down later. It looked unsanitary in its current state. Did they have any more catnip oil or salt? She shook her head. *Focus on one thing at a time.*

Stepping through the archway, her breath became heavier. Sometimes being underground in these tunnels was suffocating to her lungs, though she acclimated. They all had. At the corner of the large rectangular room was The Elder, ranting on about something to Frank with a raised voice. "Aiella" floated across the room in the conversation, giving an opportunity to interject.

"You wanted me?" Aiella asked, maneuvering her way through the cots. Why did The Elder never leave the sleeping quarters?

"Yes! Finally!" She responded loudly. Frank shot Aiella an exasperated glance before getting up to leave.

"I'll leave you to it, then," he blurted. Aiella raised her eyebrows in question, but he left them alone as he exited through the tunnel that led to the waste room. Aiella watched, amused. *The Elder's upset must have driven everyone to the communal bath*, she thought with a chuckle. Not that she blamed them. The Elder was an intense woman. Quiet mostly, but when she had something she needed to say, she made it known. Aiella shuddered, realizing that she might be in for an earful. Turning back to the lady before her, she found violet eyes glaring back at her.

"I want to leave." The Elder spoke with such clarity and force that Aiella nearly jumped. She sat down on the hard cot next to her, fidgeting with her fingernails as she looked into those fervent eyes. How was she supposed to respond to that?

"Do you hear me, child?" She spoke firmly. "I want to leave. I need to leave." The woman who rarely left the same underground dirt room she slept in suddenly wanted to leave the tunnels altogether?

"Is that what you told Frank and the others?" Aiella asked slowly. Surely this would have caused more alarm if she had.

"Of course not. Why would I tell them that? I know the answer Frank would give me. It's just a ridiculous one," she said with a huff.

"Okay... And why are you telling *me* this?" Aiella queried, narrowing her eyes. "You know I'm under the same orders as everyone else to remain here for my safety. For all of our safety. I'm only allowed once a fortnight above the surface, and that's only to gather food for everyone else." The fresh, early spring air would see her soon for exactly that reason.

"It's different with you," The Elder said bluntly. "You have more control than you think."

Aiella let out an exasperated laugh. "No," she said. "I don't." She paused before continuing. Is that what everyone in their tribe thought? "Can I ask why you want to leave?"

"No. You cannot. Just forget it," the Elder replied with another huff. Before Aiella could object, she lay back down on her cot, nudging Aiella off with her foot as she rolled over to face the grungy wall. Aiella stood up to find the others, stopping at the curtain to take another look in the old lady's direction. She was still facing the wall on her side. *Odd.* Stepping through the curtains, she sprinted across the tiny waste room to the last set of shaggy curtains in their underground house. She pulled them aside, the greetings of most of their small tribe echoing off the water to her. It was a pitiful excuse for a bath or pool.

For better or worse, this post-apocalyptic lifestyle was all they knew now. Normal was some distant fairytale.

Chapter 2

Rocks and dust formed a callus texture under Aiella's fingers as she ran them across the walls in the corridor. Their home in these tunnels was "simple" architecture, an underground basin of sorts with five distinct rooms, all linearly connected through dirt archways. It was far from simple in her opinion, but that is what Frank had described to her as he trained Aiella to keep everything running smoothly alongside him. She still didn't know why he had chosen her to do it all. Maybe that was what The Elder had meant by her differing from the others. She looked like the number two in command, but really, she was under the orders of Frank, like everyone else. There was a lot of protest that he had chosen her to trust with important tasks, such as gathering food, but she had a knack for it all that couldn't be explained. Besides, she didn't mind risking herself to keep her family safe and sound. What else was there to do? That choice was simple, at least.

Following the tunnel up a slight incline, she came upon the ladder leading up the cliff that concealed them, chills passing through her inadvertently as she thought about where it led. The ladder went through a cylindrical area just large enough for a human body to fit through, ending at the top with a trapdoor concealed by bushes and other miscellaneous plants. The surrounding stone was always sticky and humid, no matter if it was freezing or one hundred degrees out. Though she had climbed that ladder most weeks for the better part of the last decade, she still felt a knot in her gut whenever approaching it. Perhaps the ladder was a reminder of how detached from the world they had become. It was an isolated life.

As much as her mind willed her to sit right here, dwelling on her misfortunes, she knew something better awaited her above this abode. Life was short, made even shorter by malnutrition. No time for negativity right now.

Musty air found its way to her tightened lungs as she inhaled a deep breath, slinging her backpack just right so that it wouldn't impede her climb. Her spear for hunting was cumbersome. Making the ascent with the small solar panels needing to be left out for the day was always awkward enough, their sharp edges jabbing into her sides while the knife in her pocket threatened to pierce skin.

After another keen gasp, the ladder greeted her with a slick and cool touch, shivering her bones while simultaneously exhilarating her for the outside. This had been the longest stretch in a while between finding rations for the tribe, as the foreboding last leg of winter spoke. Her scaling pace quickened as she reached the trapdoor, the alternating pitter-patter of hands and feet on metal as amiable as ever. History felt engraved on the wood as she heaved it upward, her breath catching as sunlight and a cool spring breeze greeted her.

As she climbed out into the world, Aiella was careful to replace the trapdoor with debris over it. Visiting the outdoors as scarcely as she did meant she only saw each season a handful of times each year, but spring held her heart. She took in as deep a breath as her lungs would allow, refreshed as she noticed green grass and moss spreading out underneath where she stood, the snow melting away. A beautiful golden flower peeked through, its aroma dancing around Aiella as she brought it up to her cheeks. *How could a world filled with so much pure beauty ever be dangerous?*

She could remain content with the magic of nature pressed in her palm for hours, days even, but she knew she had much to get through by the time darkness hit. She wouldn't let her own selfishness impede her tribe's eating again. Quickly shuffling over the growing bushes surrounding the hidden entry, she scanned the region for the best location to set the small solar panels for the day. Not twenty feet away was a golden patch of sunlight in a clearing away from the trees. The foliage was always growing and changing, making her placement of the devices ever-changing with them.

After she set the panels down, her backpack was far more comfortable. She made her way to a pathway down the cliff that was less steep than the others, with enough trees encompassing it to feel confident she would not fall. She had found it several years before, and now it was second nature, making her way down the slope; she hardly needed the trees to keep her balance. Gripping her backpack tightly and removing the spear from on top, she effortlessly made it down the zigzagged cliffside. Thankfully, it was not muddy like it had been on her previous ventures since there was just enough frost on the ground from the shade to keep it solid. Within a few minutes, she was standing on the edge of the river, with the rushing waterfall roaring around the corner.

Walking along the water was all she would have time for, given her later-than-usual start. Before long, she found a few loganberry bushes she knew were safe for consumption. Dandelions glistened in the sunshine, and she dug those up with earnest every chance she got. There weren't many, being early in the season still, but after this many years in hiding, they knew how to make a little go a long way. During the winter, most of their food supply had to come from hunting small animals that were preserved and eating bark off trees. With the river flowing rapidly again, and plants quickly sprouting up with every step she took, Aiella was hoping for more variety. Thistle would be abundant soon, and summer would bring beautiful wild roses. For now, she knew the berries and yellow flowers would at least make the softened pine bark taste much less like dust and more like a dessert.

When she had a large cloth filled with them alongside some blackberries, she found the largest pine tree near her and scraped at it with the side of her pocket knife she had tucked away in her waist. She took a deep breath, lowering her knife to the bark. It was tougher on the outside than she expected, and splintering pain cut through her as she nicked the flesh of the tree too deeply. It was as if she could hear the soul of the tree singing out in pain. Aiella's vision blurred, her fingers tightening around the handle of her weapon as she threw herself onto the ground away from the tree, her knees instinctively pulling themselves into her chest.

Lightning seemed to shock her entire body as she rocked back and forth, and the surrounding scenery looked duller as her eyesight cleared. Swallowing, she stood up slowly, approaching the tree for the second time. She winced as she began scraping, anxiously awaiting the pain that didn't come again. Heaving a sigh of relief, the agony lay dormant.

After carefully exposing the inner flesh, she worked methodically, slicing as many large, thin strips as she could before her hand cramped up. These could be lightly roasted, or boiled to make them softer and more diverse. Gazing overhead through the tree line, the sun was still high in the sky. If she had to guess, she had been out here for a few hours already, and presumably had the same amount of daylight left. Allowing her cheek to rest against the cool, newly exposed bark, she inhaled the fresh air. Spring licked at her face, the essence spreading deeper into her and giving her an energy like no other. She dutifully finished peeling from the giving plant, then let her instincts carry her to the water.

Scurrying to the river's edge, a girl with flowing, long hair and both a blue and gold eye stared back at her. She emanated earthy tones from her rosy cheeks to her tanned skin, her hair as dark as the ground she was standing on, accented in the sun by fiery red. She smiled upon seeing a handful of large fish in a pocket of the shallow water. Those alone could sustain them for the next week or two. Aiella waded into the icy stream, doing her best not to shiver and scare the catch away. She took aim and released.

The small, damp corridor revealing the entrance to the living area was filled with shouting when Aiella returned from her successful day of hunting and gathering. Her arms ached tremendously, the weight of the now-charged solar panels and the variety of meats and plants more than she had gathered in a while. There was a giddy bounce to her step, elation at providing for the tribe filling her soul. Lost in thought, her foot caught on a small hole in the hardened dirt floor, almost sending her flying.

"They're right, Frank," she heard Alta speaking in a calm voice on the other side of the curtains. The voices of all the other middle-aged residents formed a cacophony of opinions after yelling their agreement. Aiella bit her lip, her back and feet now screaming alongside her tired arms. These arguments were rare, but still never fun to be a part of. Maybe the charged panels would help? They could use none of their few electronics for a good chunk of time now, after all.

As she was about to pull aside the curtain with her leg, she froze, the dim lighting from the other room creeping onto her body through the cracks in the material.

"Aiella gets to leave every other week and safely returns each time." She recognized Philip's voice and rolled her eyes. Typical of him.

"That's true, but—"

"There are no buts, Frank," Darian interjected.

"You've never known what you were doing, so why do we listen to you still after all these years?" Milan hissed. Well, that was enough. Throwing the thick curtain to the side, Aiella waltzed into the room with her head held confidently.

"The panels are now charged, so we can connect them to your devices to replenish. I've also gathered enough food for the next fortnight." She gestured to Frank, who immediately followed her through the overcrowded room into the cooking quarters.

"Your timing is impeccable," he said with an exhausted sigh. "There is practically a mutiny on our hands out there." His brows furrowed as he wiped at beads of sweat with the back of his arm.

"What sparked this?" She asked, heaving her bag onto the countertop. As he spoke, she interrupted him. "Actually, hang on. Let me bring them these first." She carefully slid each of the panels out of her bag, cradling them in her arms.

"I'll start sorting through these goodies," he told her. She nodded in response, turning back towards the entrance to the living room.

"Ella?" Frank said after a moment, regaining her full attention. She spun back around. "You're a natural," he told her, seeing everything unloaded onto their counter.

"Thanks," Aiella chuckled. "It really comes pretty easily these days. Aside from that cougar, of course. It's all thanks to you." Frank beamed. "I can go out and cook these over a fire in a bit if I need to?" Mentally, she crossed her fingers.

"Oh no, we have plenty of options in here. Could salt it and eat it as is. The fish will be fine, being so freshly caught. We could use something different around here. I am glad that the river is brimming again! The bark can be boiled... Ah, well, I suppose the meat could as well..." Frank trailed off, still excited about the same culinary experiences he had been giving them for years. He was an engineer back before the ceremotosis outbreak, but with how apt he was in their sad excuse for a kitchen, no one would ever guess it.

Using her foot to maneuver the curtain aside, she was met with frosty glares from almost everyone in the main living area. Leaning against the wall opposite her was Eli, a slight smirk on his face when he saw her, but otherwise watching the scene unfold indifferently as usual.

"Here," she told them plainly, setting the panels down gently at the center of the room. Nobody spoke a word, but ignored her and began talking amongst themselves about who would get to use the few pieces of technology they had first. "Don't worry, you don't need to thank me or anything."

"You're right about that, young lady," Milan snickered with crossed arms. She was sitting on one of the old, ripped recliners, though it never reclined properly anymore. For a moment, Aiella hoped it would fall back and snap, just enough to startle the old hag.

"Oh, please, hardly any of this is her fault," Alta retorted from next to her, giving a curt nod in Aiella's direction.

"Like heck it is!" Milan raised her voice, leaning forward out of the chair. "If Frank wasn't so set on replacing the daughter he lost by favoring her constantly, we might have a shot at actually doing something outside for ourselves! Besides, she was the one The Elder was so adamant about talking to!" The entire room stilled in icy silence. Aiella remained rooted to the spot she was in, unsure of how to respond. Was it true? Did he give her these responsibilities only because he missed the daughter he never got to see grow up? That didn't seem fair or like Frank. She bowed her head, knives cutting through her heart, to think that the people she considered family thought so low of her. *And wait—The Elder?*

"Ahem," Dimitri cleared his throat, glancing behind Aiella's head. She watched Lara wrap herself around his right arm, anticipating the confrontation to come.

"How could you say that, Milan?" Frank demanded, his presence enclosing like a dense fog around them all. Across the room, Eli raised an eyebrow and flicked his head to his left, signaling for Aiella to join him. She scampered between two beaten-down sofas, everyone too fixated on Frank now to care what she was doing.

"That was cold," Knox said, whistling in disapproval. He knew too well what it was like to lose a wife and child. His brother-in-law, Adler, gave a dramatic, sympathetic nod.

"Milan's got some loose wires up there, I'll say," Eli whispered as she leaned against the cool wall next to him.

"Something like that," she muttered, noticing the comforting feeling of his warm breath on the top of her head.

"Hey," he said, leaning down closer to her. "What did you snag for food?" The normalcy of the question made Aiella smile widely, a mirrored grin spreading across Eli's face as well.

"You're too much," she told him, laughing quietly.

"What?" he asked innocently, pointing to his chest. "Me? Never."

"I can't believe you would put my family's death into the reasoning that I let someone else try to run this place with me," Frank said, his voice threatened to crack.

"She isn't even eighteen yet. She is a child!" Milan objected.

"Why would age matter in a time like this?" Frank yelled back. Aiella scanned the room, realizing Luke and Alexis were the only two not present. And The Elder, but that was nothing new.

"Where are Alexis and Luke?" She asked Eli under her breath.

"Ah, that's only part of why this whole thing started," he explained.

"What? Why? Where are they?" Aiella whispered. Eli turned his attention back to the confrontation before them.

"She goes out there as often as we need and gathers the supplies and provisions for you all. To help me. To help us. You don't have to do anything except sit in here and survive, so why does it even matter?" Frank's hands balled into fists by his side, his ears and cheeks reddening to a point where, in the soft light of the lanterns, they looked almost black or purple.

"I think they just all want to make their own choices. Fend for themselves. See the real world again," Alta responded, trying to play mediator.

"*They*? Or *you*?" Frank asked, obviously taken aback. Alta dropped her head, answering with no need to speak.

"Would this be a bad time to ask you out on a date?" Eli questioned. Aiella could smack him.

"Are you kidding me?" She hissed. "You didn't even answer my question."

"If I had, would you have answered mine?" He implored.

"What in the world happened today, Eli?" she insisted. Everyone around them was arguing profusely.

"Well," he said, shifting on the wall to face her more directly. Her stomach clenched a bit. "You see, they had their own little date, it would seem," he whispered, an entertained smile breaking out on his lips again. Aiella stared back at him blankly, knowing he was thinking of them on a date. Part of her was, too, just not the part that would ever follow through.

"And...?" she asked, though unsure if he would hear through all the shouting going on.

"Frank found them at the waterfall window. At first, we thought they had left like The Elder. They weren't doing anything, just—"

"Aiella is immune to the disease!" Frank yelled.

Chapter 3

"Did we miss something?" Luke asked as he walked into the room, breaking the silence. Alexis was next to him, her fingers interlaced with his as they walked through the thin barrier leading to the corridors. Aiella gawked, her insides in turmoil from too many things happening all at once.

"The Elder is missing?" Aiella asked quietly. All she could think about was the conversation she had had with her before. She had been adamant about leaving. Aiella never told Frank, but maybe she should have. Was this her fault?

Frank groaned, rubbing his forehead with his eyes clenched shut, something he only did in deep concentration or frustration. Aiella reckoned it stemmed from both feelings right now.

"Did you know?" Eli asked her quietly, placing a hand gently on her shoulder. About their missing family member or her immunity? She simply shook her head, unable to form words.

No one else seemed to have the words either. Not even Milan or Devon.

"Come here," Eli whispered, pulling her into a protective hug. For once, she didn't shield her feelings and pull away.

"Are you guys okay?" Alexis asked in a low voice, walking up beside them.

"What's going on?" Luke questioned a bit too audibly. Frank glanced up at them through his fingers, running his other hand through his silver hair. Aiella pulled away from Eli, straightening her posture. No point in shying away from the inevitable.

"What do you mean, I am immune?" She asked him in a scratchy voice. Was it just her, or was the room getting smaller?

Frank exhaled deeply, walking further towards the center of the dim room. The ceiling was filled with cracks, and the lanterns were unreliable at best. Though the ventilation system was functional, the air quality was still less than ideal, filled with dirt particles and recycled breaths. Everything was a shade of gray or brown from sitting underground for so long.

"You always have been," he told Aiella directly. He cleared his throat, addressing the rest of the group as well. "That's why she has been the one to do all the hunting and gathering for so long. That's why I have trained her. I do not know if the outdoor world is safe from the fire again yet, but of course, I want us all to be free. Of course I want us all to venture out, and not live in fear, but... I was told she can't catch it or even carry it when The Elder came with her. She was adamant about it. Ella is immune to ceremotosis."

"The Elder never told me she was the one who brought me here," Aiella spoke softly.

"I think there is a lot that the old bat didn't tell you. Or any of us! Like, where did she go? When did she even leave?" Devon bellowed to them all. Aiella was at a loss, as was Frank.

"I don't know," Frank said slowly, shaking his head. "Ella, did you see any signs of her while you were out today?" A flicker of hope flittered briefly in everyone's eyes. She merely shook her head.

Useless.

The Elder had brought her here? And knew she was immune? Why did she call herself *The Elder*, anyway? *Why did she leave?* How had no one seen this? With her head spinning, Aiella shut her eyes to block out the fuzzies blurring her vision. She tried to piece everything together, but it was futile, and she felt her body tumbling towards the ground as darkness consumed her.

The Elder.

Immune.

Aiella groaned, a hand immediately on her arm.

"She's up!" Eli shouted. "Are you okay?" Aiella opened her eyes again to find him smiling at her, clearly relieved.

"What in the world just happened?" She muttered, letting him gently pull her into a sitting position.

"Here's some water," Frank told her, handing a copper bottle to her after he rushed across the room.

"Thanks," she murmured, placing it to her lips. What a day. Looking around, she was glad to see everyone else had cleared out of the living area. How long was she passed out for?

"It's late," Eli said with a chuckle. "They are all in bed."

"Alexis and Luke, too?" She asked. He gave an amusing nod.

"Thought they cared about you more, huh?" He teased. Aiella rolled her eyes, playfully shoving him aside.

"If the only one who cares about me is you, I'm in trouble." She grinned, her head clearing more.

"Nah, I'm all—"

"Eli, could you give us a minute?" Frank interrupted.

"Yes," he replied, clearing his throat. "Of course." He jumped back to his feet and was gone through the curtain, Frank's eyes fixated on Aiella as she watched Eli leave the room, her lips drawn tightly shut. She had nothing to say to him right now. Not nice, at least. Silence awkwardly draped over the air.

"Are you okay?" he finally asked.

"Fine," she said, not making eye contact.

"I know you're probably upset..."

"Upset?" She scoffed. "That's an understatement. Why didn't you tell me?" She spat. "I am way more than upset." She paused for a moment while more anger boiled deep inside her. "All this time, I believed I was at just as much risk. You let them believe it! They probably feel just as betrayed as I do right now." Her eyes burned, blurring again as she swallowed down the lump rising in her throat. So much for staying quiet. It had never been her strong suit, though she never felt confident in what she had to say either.

"Ella, I know you're mad at me—"

"Yup."

"—but I kept it from you before because I didn't want to scare you. Or worse, have you believe something that ended up being false." He sat down next to her on the earthy floor. She pulled her knees to her chest, looking in the opposite direction from him.

"They trust you, Frank. We all trust you." Many of them had heartbreaking experiences before gathering here. The death of their loved ones, their lives destroyed. They all had unique stories, but their differences didn't matter when their losses were the same. They all had a gaping hole within them, and no one knew how to cope until they found Frank.

And Frank had been keeping secrets.

"Ella..."

"How much have you been keeping from us? From *ME*?" She raised her voice, violently whipping her head and body around to face him.

"Nothing, Ella. Just that." He tried reaching an arm to her shoulder, but she yanked it away, standing up.

"I don't believe you," she hissed, turning to leave for bed.

"Ella, wait!" he pleaded. "I was worried. I still am. After losing my family..." He whispered, choking on the words. She turned around, walking back over to him slowly. He took a moment to regain his composure before standing and continuing.

"You are like a daughter to me. I just didn't want you to get hurt. Not physically or emotionally. I don't know how you're immune, or how The Elder knows. There are still so many unknowns, and

I just didn't want to expose you to all of them when you were younger. I kind of thought The Elder would just tell you herself if what she said was true. But she kept it to herself. Barely talking, barely interacting with anyone, and now she is gone. *Why is she gone?*" He rubbed his temples as he paced the room. Aiella realized something bigger was clearly at play.

"Would you ever have told me if everyone hadn't baited it out of you?" She asked quietly.

There was a long pause before Frank answered her. "Yes," he said slowly, "especially now that The Elder is gone. I always felt it wasn't my secret to tell. But with her missing..."

"I don't think it was ever anyone's secret to keep," she responded bluntly. "This is *my* life we are talking about."

"Aiella, I'm sorry," he whispered, his eyes misty. Taking the few steps needed, he wrapped her in a fatherly hug. She didn't object, though a part of her bitterly wanted to.

"The Elder is really missing?" She asked, her voice quivering.

"Yes," he whispered back.

"I'm scared, Frank," she admitted.

"Me too," he confessed, pulling back to look at her. "I am rather glad that you know now, though. About your immunity. Quite a weight off these big old shoulders." He chuckled, and Aiella immediately felt her body destressing.

"What should we do about The Elder?" Aiella asked, hoping he would have some kind of plan.

"Come sit," he encouraged, plopping down on the old sofa. While they had little down here compared to what people had before the outbreak, it was still cozy. Maybe they had all grown too accustomed to this mundane life, but sometimes she could convince herself it wasn't half bad.

As Aiella took a seat next to him, she appreciated the couches had been sanitized when they were first brought with their inhabitants years and years ago, even though they were now worn and mismatched. The result was something reminiscent of what Aiella believed an old lounge or bar would have looked like back in the 1900s. Not glamorous like the late 21st century looked from photos, and there was no smoke circling men's heads like they supposedly was in the 20th century. The dust that always lingered could pass as the same, though. It was hard to know for sure, but she imagined.

"I miss beanbags," she heard Frank mutter to himself.

"What is that?" she asked him. He swiftly brushed off the question and turned the focus back to her. She felt as though she was under interrogation for something and wasn't sure why. "Is there something else going on? Something bigger?" Aiella inquired. "There is, isn't there? Do you have a plan to save The Elder? It's not safe out there for her, especially not at night."

Frank shook his head, fixated on a spot across the room, though it was apparent that he was not looking at anything. When he finally spoke, it was slow and soft: "I am curious if maybe you have any memories of your mom before she died from the disease." He paused for a moment, likely to see if she had anything to add. She did not.

"I've just always wondered how you're immune." He looked at her, skeptical but hopeful. She was having a hard time imagining her immunity being of much more help than it already was to them.

"Where are we going with this?" She asked, her body fighting fatigue, though her mind was restless.

"I know The Elder knew your mother, too. Maybe it could help us find her?" Frank suggested. "I figured this new information might trigger questions about your mom, too."

"My mom? What about my mom? I was only...what? Two when I was brought here? She caught ceremotosis and died the same fiery death as everyone else," she conceded wearily. She desperately wanted to help find the oldest member of their adoptive family, but she couldn't remember life before all of this. Her mom. Her home. She had no recollection of what that had been like, but she liked to imagine that they had a fence around the backyard, with flowers and trees lining the property. Maybe there was a pond...

"Ella," Frank said quietly, "we are in charge of our own happiness. That is something I push heavily. But there are so many questions I have had since you arrived here. Your being immune gives us hope."

"Hope? How is there hope? Can you really expect to save the world, just the fourteen of us? Assuming The Elder is even still alive by the time we find her." Saying it out loud made it feel dreadfully unrealistic.

"We cannot blindly assume there is no one out there. Hope is all we have. Don't you want Alexis and Luke to have the best life they can while they have it?" he pressed. "Don't you want to learn about your past?"

"Asking questions we can't find answers to is pointless, Frank," she responded disheartened. "I go back and forth with this every single day, and it eats me up. But I don't remember my parents, and I don't know why I am immune. I always suspected I was, but I just don't know the answer. Did I get sick once already? Did I get through an ailment that no one else did? That seems unlikely, and why I am immune doesn't matter. I just am, and I don't think I want to remember my past. I want only everyone here to have a wonderful future." She dropped her head; defeat threatened her eyes.

"Okay," Frank whispered. "The only question we will focus on right now is where one member of our family went." Aiella nodded, and with a pat on the head, he trudged away, leaving her to her thoughts.

What was the point of this life they all had? What was the point if they knew they wouldn't be able to continue on with new generations? Sure, there were enough people in the tunnels to start a small civilization again. She was confident there were a few sets of couples that would be more than eager for that freedom. But these tunnels could not hold growing families. Even the backup tunnels concealed far past the ladder couldn't do that. They were simply meant to provide temporary housing in a time of crisis. And time was running out.

For all they knew, they were the last humans in the country, possibly even the world. Technology had crashed so fast when the disease had its initial outbreak that many across the states didn't even know what was coming. They had relied on something virtual for so long that one crack surfaced in the system and they were all torn apart. Society collapsed faster than anyone could have foreseen.

She remembered Frank describing the events years ago, told her, "It was as if you took all the dangerous diseases we learned about in school and made them one. It ate you alive. First you blistered, then you burned."

And she was immune to it.

Her chest tightened. How unfair that she didn't have to suffer the same fate so many had. The massive amount of pain was so intense that even those who merely witnessed it were healing from wounds years and years later.

Everything was tied to her immunity, even though she didn't want to admit it.

She sat still on the couch for hours. Sleep came in and out, interrupted by lucid images. Aiella pictured the sun peeking through the windows they didn't have and felt a gut-wrenching sorrow. For herself, for Frank, for Luke and Alexis, who had hardly ever seen the world in all their lives, and for the others too. It was unfair that she got to experience it, even if only for a couple of days a month. It gave her a reason to keep trudging on. What was the motivation for everyone else each day? The question made her sick to her stomach.

At some point, she considered crawling into bed, but her body was too numb. Though it felt impossible, a solution had to exist for all of them to live more normal lives, like those that half of them watched wither away before them. As morning crept up, she had an energy surging through her as powerful as the trees sprouting their new leaves.

The tiniest ember of hope started burning, and it couldn't be extinguished.

She was the only one who could go save The Elder. Wherever, or however far she may be. Aiella was the only one who could find her and bring her home. The only one who could get the answers from her that Frank needed.

She was going to leave.

Chapter 4

The motion was always the same. Everyone grumbled into the kitchen area to grab their rations for the day. There were always similar dishes, if you could call them that. They were always small and ready at the same time each morning. Everyone took their portions, and it was up to them how to eat them throughout the day. It had been years since anyone had tried to share.

Her tribe looked bored and barely alive. The light burning in their eyes was nearly extinguished, with only looks of disdain given to Aiella. Every one of them was thin and paler than their skin colors should have been, even from what she could see from the limited lighting. A few were reading books, the same ones they had read a dozen times, while others were fidgeting with some of the old broken technology they had brought in. The rest were mindlessly chewing their small portions of food, looking more like wild animals than humans. Hope was dwindling, and in that moment, Aiella was positive she was making the right choice in leaving, no matter how much it terrified her.

No one wanted her here.

Her head spinning, she left to find a tiny shred of privacy. She was walking through the curtain to go use the waste room when she paused, looking back behind her at the cots, all empty. Just then, she heard a faint voice coming from her right. She stopped walking to listen more closely. Faint whispers were coming from inside the waste room. She walked in, but there was no one there.

"Shhh!" Alexis giggled.

"I can't help it; you *are* beautiful," Luke replied.

Aiella tiptoed across the waste room, stifling a giggle herself, pulling the curtain to the community pool open. Before her were the two entangled in the water, their clothes sopping wet. She watched, speechless and entertained, as she continued to walk quietly into the room. Luke leaned in.

Her tiptoeing came to a halt as she slipped and made a splashing sound on the damp floor.

Both Luke and Alexis froze mid-kiss.

Aiella laughed as she walked to them across the room.

"I need to talk to you both," Aiella said with a chuckle. "Not about this, don't worry," she added, gesturing at them. "I am happy for you both, to be fair." A snort came out. "You have more of a life than I do now. More of a love life too, for sure." She keeled over with exasperated laughter. Alexis and Luke just looked at each other. She was losing her mind.

Aiella regained her composure, clearing her throat. "I'm leaving for food soon, and Frank is already extremely stressed… I just wanted to tell you to take it easy and not cause trouble while I am gone."

"When have we ever caused an issue?" Luke asked stubbornly. She raised an eyebrow.

"Really?" she asked. "We have *all* been challenging this week." The other two gave a shrug of agreement, humorous grins playing across their mouths.

"Listen…" Aiella started in a lower voice, "I know how hard it is. How hard it is to feel like prisoners trapped down here. But it is the only way we know we can all keep surviving right now. We could be some of the last humans there are. We owe it to the future to keep ourselves alive." She stopped, letting her words sink in for a moment. Their somber faces looking back at her in the dim lighting reflected that she had accomplished just that. She didn't want to think about if The Elder was found deceased, but if she was, she had to give her the honor of bringing her body home, or at least giving a proper burial.

"Why are you telling us this ahead of time?" Alexis pondered. "I would guess this was Frank's idea after the last food scare?"

Aiella shifted uncomfortably. "Er… I'm not telling Frank," she admitted. The others stifled a gasp as she rushed the rest out. "There is just so much going on in his head already that I don't want to get his hopes up too," she babbled. "Or worse, disappoint him. He does so much for everyone, and has already lost so much." She hung her head, upset with herself for holding a secret. "He will be concerned if I am not back within a day or two," she continued, "But I need you two to make sure he doesn't come after me." They all shivered together.

"Ella? Why would it take you more than just a day trip? You never do more than a day trip," Luke stated, concern dripping from his tone.

"It probably won't," she lied. They looked at each other nervously. Aiella told herself it was just a normal hunting day trip. Just one she was sneaking out for. She shouldn't have told them anything at all. She was always better off alone, especially now. Secretly, she hoped they would try to change her mind about leaving behind Frank's back.

They didn't.

The evening before she was preparing to leave was a difficult one. It took everything in her to act as though everything was normal. To act like tomorrow, she would simply go out hunting for some small rabbits, to gather some berries. In reality, she didn't know how far she would have to go from home to look for their lost member. If she remembered correctly, the fallen ghost city of Spokane should be southeast of her, about a four-to-five-hour walk. She sighed, not even knowing where to begin. She wasn't sure how much she could trust her memory of the whereabouts since she had only been once, years before. Regardless, if The Elder couldn't be found near here, hopefully, she wasn't further than four or five hours away. Of course, searching that far radius meant...

Too much. It meant too much.

She had to hope she was nearby or in the fallen city. She couldn't search any more than that. It wasn't possible alone. Why was she even leaving? She should stay here. Her heart skipped a beat knowing there was a real possibility she would never return. Even being as used to it as she was, the wild was... Well, wild. She could easily be dead in a few days.

Eli was shifting against the wall, watching her. All six feet of him looked fragile and soft, his eyebrows furrowed deeply and his hands tapped quietly on his thighs. Did he know what she was really going to do? Had he been listening in on her conversations? For a brief moment, she realized perhaps she should let him in on it. She knew inevitably he would insist on coming along, though, so threw that idea away immediately. In no way would she put him in danger. This was her sacrifice to make.

"You seem to be preparing for some kind of little excursion," he said with a chuckle, walking to her side. Aiella casually brushed a hair out of her face, trying not to tense up. There was no way he knew her plan.

"Weather right now can be unpredictable," she replied with a shrug. "I'm just getting ready in advance for whenever I go out next." He narrowed his eyes at her, nodding slowly.

"Hmm. I see." He took another step closer to her, though, his eyebrows softening. "Are you okay?" he asked gently, tucking the last stray hair of hers behind her ear. She immediately felt them reddening, her stomach somersaulting.

"What do you mean?" She responded quietly.

"I mean, you just found out some pretty big news in front of everyone," he said with a laugh. Leave it to him to pinpoint exactly what was going through her thoughts.

"Eli..." she said slowly, placing her fists on his chest, watching her fingers as they slowly opened on his shirt. She never wanted them to settle on each other just because they were the only ones their age down here, but he was undoubtedly her best friend.

"Promise me you will let nothing happen to Luke and Alexis," she whispered, still staring at her hands square on his chest.

"What? Why wouldn't you?" He questioned.

"If something ever happened to me. Or to Frank. Or to both of us. Mostly me," she scrambled.

"Nothing is going to happen to you, Ella," he murmured. The tone of his voice almost had her believing it.

"I'm scared, Eli," she confessed gingerly. Without pressing for more, he wrapped his arms around her in a friendly, protective hug, the foreboding task before her momentarily forgotten.

Later, when she entered the kitchen to set her supplies together for her trip, she was surprised to see Frank.

"Everyone seemed to either be relaxing in the pool or in the living room," she told him, nodding her head towards the curtains on her left. He was leaning over the counter, a pondering mist in his eyes as he smiled at her.

"Hoped to be alone?"

"No, of course not," she blurted. Maybe too quickly. She inhaled to slow her defenses. "You just looked distressed... Or something. I'm just surprised you aren't with Alta." Frank gave out a low chuckle, clutching his hands together as he bent and shook his head.

"I miss my wife and kiddo," he breathed.

"I'm so sorry, Frank. If I could go back in time and let them have my immunity, I would. For you." She placed the objects she was carrying down in the corner and gave him a soft side hug. "I'd do anything for this makeshift family we have now," she added. He nodded, standing up and giving her a brief hug before leaning his back against the other counter behind him. She looked at him quizzically.

"You know, sometimes that's what worries me."

"What do you mean?" She asked, her hair on her neck standing up.

"Anything else you would like to discuss before heading out to scavenge tomorrow?" He asked her. She shook her head, Frank giving out a low whistle.

"You know?" She asked when what he had just mentioned sank in.

"Of course I know. I'm fine with it, though. You could've just asked me instead of hiding it, you know. Nothing wrong with wanting to stock up on rations after those hunger pangs a few weeks back." She let out a deep exhale, glad she wouldn't have to sneak out now. The deceit would be easier once she was far away. "Just remember, dear Ella, our happiness is the only thing we are fully in control of." He walked over to her and whispered, "I'm so proud of you." Then he kissed her on the forehead. "I'm going to retire early tonight, I think."

"Sounds good," she told him with a smile. "Have sweet dreams."

"You too, my dear girl." He smiled in return and walked out of the room to bed. Aiella heaved a sigh of relief while finishing putting everything together for the morning, doing her best to ignore the knots forming in her stomach.

Chapter 5

"You know I get nervous about you leaving every time," Frank told her with a hug.

"It's the fatherly instinct," she smiled, guilt overcoming her, knowing she was hiding things from him. He went back to the kitchen, a lingering frown on his face.

Eli walked through the curtains almost instantaneously after Frank had left through them. Everyone else was still sleeping, including Alexis and Luke. They knew her plan and had said goodbye last night at the ends of the tunnels, long after everyone else was sleeping.

"Be safe, Aiella," Eli said quietly, interjecting her thoughts. For the first time in a while, she realized how hurt he might be that she had been rejecting him time and time again. The jokes, the snide comments—they were all a facade. Fueled by the fear that she had not been out this long on her own, she hastened to him and hugged him. It was brief, but far more intimate than any other in the past, his surprisingly muscular arms enveloping her as he breathed in her hair. She pulled back, but her body betrayed her mind, longing for more.

"I could come with you," he murmured, his eyes shut, his arm reaching out for her to come back into his embrace.

"You can't," she whispered, but she slipped back into his arms. She inhaled the scent of his skin, a comforting blend of both musty and fresh. "I'm sorry. I'll be safe," she said into his chest. He gave her one big squeeze that she returned before pulling away.

This is like any other food trip, she told herself, focusing on the energy that climbing the rope ladder to the earth's surface gave her. She trembled as she lifted the heavy door, and what she saw on the other side was worth the effort and strain. It was always worth it. Climbing out, she took the first deep breath of fully fresh air she had in just shy of a week. A week too long. The trees were fuller, flowers more in bloom than they had been before. The ground below her seemed to grow brighter as she watched it, an unexplainable energy surging through her entire soul. She ached for the rest of her family below her as she closed the door and took in her surroundings, trying to orient herself in the early twilight.

She got chills down her back as she started making her way through the trees, knowing that most of her trek today would be entirely through heavy forest. There was a cool breeze sweeping through the woods, birds echoing their songs to each other on the hunt for a mate. Aiella wished she could lie down and relax for even a few hours, but like every time she stepped outdoors, she knew too much was at stake not to always have a heightened sense of awareness. She let her determination push her past her fears, and she walked on, taking in the scenery around every twist and turn as she headed in the opposite direction she usually did. She hoped she could find some berries or other fruit along her path today, and just before dark, be able to spear a fish to cook over a fire for dinner. As she tossed and turned all night in bed, she decided she would first go to the old city of Spokane, and then take her time looking around closer to home if she did not find The Elder there. Might as well get the most challenging area out of the way first and then work backwards. She thought it seemed unlikely The Elder had gone that far, so she figured if she beat her to a destination, she could circle back and find her. It felt like flawed logic; truthfully, she wanted to find a unique city trinket of a sort for Alexis and Luke back home. If she ever returned home. The thought made her insides twist.

Her legs were sore by the time the sun was directly overhead, and she cursed she wasn't more physically in shape. Sometimes, she dreamed about leaving the tribe altogether, and now, knowing she was safe from the terrible disease out here anyway, she imagined what it would be like to live in solitude inside these gloriously beautiful mountains. It was too painful to consider leaving behind those she loved, though. Every time she ventured out, she always went back to her underground jail cell where her family was, and this time would be no different.

She had found nothing, no signs of food or The Elder, along the varying creeks she was following throughout the day, much to her dismay. Her body grumbled. Her strength was barely adequate to get over the hills in the dense trees that the river water made look so easy to climb. When the air chilled again, and it seemed the forest was opening up into space a bit below her, she knew she had been faultless in her instinct of which direction to go, though it had taken her longer than she had relied on. She needed to catch and prepare her own dinner before it became dark. Her resources would be scarce without as many trees.

The colors bursting through the clouds in the sky were enough to make anyone feel giddy and warm, and Aiella looked around her, considering where to take shelter for the night. Up ahead, closer to the edge of the forest, there was a cluster of trees where another had fallen over them. She grabbed her belongings and the fish ready to be cooked and headed in that direction. Fifteen minutes later, she was looking inside a large hollowed-out log. *This will have to do*, she thought. Luck must be on her side, after all; she doubted she had the energy to build any type of shelter quickly. It would be uncomfortable to sleep in such a tight fit, but it would suffice.

She set what she was carrying inside the log with a sigh of relief, taking a deep breath before she looked for small pieces of wood and brush to start a fire. She counted herself fortunate that she would not have to find stones or flint to start it, as years ago she had stumbled upon a fire starter she had since kept tucked into her pocket. Before long, her arms were full of what doubled as logs for a fire, and she set them down cabin style as Frank had shown her. Throwing some brush on top and clearing everything around it with her feet to keep it controlled, she had a burning flame in hardly any time at all. She sloppily placed her trout directly on top of the fire and sat to watch the sunset.

A wolf howl far in the distance chilled her to the bone, waking Aiella abruptly and adding to her eerie discomfort from the humidity that had seeped relentlessly into her. The softened log had formed to the contours of her body, begging its guest to stay with it. It took her a moment to orient herself, the sky still dark, but the slightest of breezes across Aiella's face reminded her of the mission she was on. Crawling out of the old tree trunk, she searched for signs of leftover hot coals. Guzzling water she had boiled clean last night, she silently prayed it might help her stomach from demanding more food. The forest was so thick with dark green pines; it was nearly impossible to notice anything further about her whereabouts until the sun had fully risen.

Moist, fallen pine needles circled their aromas to Aiella, a sudden urge to sit down on the earth overtaking her. She sat cross-legged on the cool ground, breathing deeply, contemplating heading to the city before sunrise so that she could return home faster. Her heart skipped a beat, thinking of the worry Frank and Eli would exhibit. If she could get there before dawn, she could head back to this area to camp by late afternoon.

Something was keeping her rooted to this spot, no matter how much it sounded like a solid plan to continue her expedition now. Shutting her eyes, it was easy to pretend that the world was bright and bustling around her. The sun was shining, a light breeze blowing her wild, dark auburn curls around her wind-lashed face. Flowers sprouted to the height of her hips, their sweet petals dancing in the wind while children's laughter filled the air. She smiled at the thought, grabbing dirt in her palms as she continued to imagine Earth's best.

Crack. She opened her eyes, looking off in the distance towards the city with a twinge of fear. There was something sinister about absolute darkness, especially when she knew that once upon a time it had been buzzing constantly with thousands and thousands of people and machines. The silence was suffocating.

Crack. The second, closer sound of a branch breaking behind her snapped her attention back to the present. Quietly, she slid back into her hidden shelter, daring not to breathe in case it was another dangerous animal. She peeked out slowly, exhaling in relief as the shadow of a small rodent skipped across her vision. Before she could realize what was happening, a graceful, silent creature came and swooped it up, giving a hoot afterward. She shivered, endless thoughts about the circle of life and the dark beauty of this world hitting her all at once. It would be best to stay concealed until the sun came up.

She must have fallen asleep again, for when Aiella opened her eyes, it was bright and sunny. Grabbing her belongings in a rushed manner, she was half tempted to sprint the rest of her journey, ultimately deciding that would be a waste of energy that she desperately needed to shuffle through an entire city *and* try to find somewhere safe to sleep again, all in one day. She resolved into a brisk stride, stopping momentarily to bend over where the fire had been before. It looked as though where she had been sitting was home to a compacted little farm of dandelions, forming a circle around the outline the weight of her body had left in the earth.

"I'm sorry, little beauties," she told the flowers, delicately holding one by the bud, "I hope I didn't squish any of you." With a grin, she continued, remembering the first time she remembered seeing one of these flowers that Frank claimed were invasive weeds.

"What is this?" Aiella asked, cocking her head curiously to one side.

"Ah. Those little invaders are weeds! Growing everywhere they aren't meant to grow."

"They look like they are supposed to be here," she replied innocently, giddily picking a bunch for herself.

Frank chuckled. "Well, if you say so. Nature has a way of doing what it needs to do, I suppose." He stepped over closer to her before gasping aloud. "That is the biggest dandelion I have ever seen!" He shouted in shock.

"A dandy-lion?" Aiella repeated, the flower the same size as two of her fists.

"Yes," Frank confirmed quietly, mesmerized by something he used to find pesky. It was Aiella's turn to giggle.

The hardest part of her walk was over. Outlines of deteriorating buildings flooded her line of vision like waves crashing onto a ship. Everything looked so dull and broken in contrast with the gorgeous scenery surrounding the city. Pain tugged firmly at her heartstrings, willing her to cry as she thought of all the people who used to call this place home. Families that no longer existed. They could no longer pass even their stories down as legacies, the only thing anyone truly ever had to leave behind.

Eventually, she found herself at the center of what once was a bustling, well-known city on the river. The dam had still lasted, so she could hear a waterfall off in the distance. She stopped walking, taking it all in, trying to decide where to find signs of The Elder. She made her way through the streets closest to the water, finding comfort in nature. A small dock lay broken to bits down below, and windows sat shattered in front of her. Somehow, though, even while destroyed, the city was breathtaking.

Aiella strolled through the once-stores, drawing in her mind how it must have felt to come here when it was at its best. A bird tweeted above her, stealing her attention. Just then, the sky quickly became engulfed in a blinding red light originating south of her. Losing her balance, she shrieked, feeling as though a jolt of lightning had just crackled through every cell within her.

Her foot crashed through the glass beneath her weight, and she cried out in pain. Alas, as quickly as the shock came, it disappeared. *What in the world was that?* Taking off her flimsy shoe, she could see blood seeping out from under her heel. Frantically searching around her to see what she could wrap it with, she spotted what looked like an old handkerchief on the dusty countertop across the street. She half walked, half hopped her way over, a bell ringing as she entered the new storefront, the sound echoing off the vacant roads. The piece of cloth was filthy, so she slapped it against her leg in an attempt to clean it off. Mostly satisfied, she wrapped it around the back of her foot and up her ankle—her toes were the only thing exposed. Careful not to step on anything else, she made her way back to her lost shoe. Before she could reach the streets, though, she froze in terror.

Books she had read, and stories Frank had told her, had her confident that what she was looking at was a vehicle of sorts. A truck from the 21st century, most likely. She had seen them broken down at points before, but never on an actual road inside a city, and never making noises. Instinctively, she forced herself to drop and crawl onto the floor. A few feet away was a concealed view of the abandoned road. Trying to be as silent as an owl, she made her way across the dusty wood, pulling herself up more with her arms. She blinked her eyes, sure that her vision must betray her. It had to be a truck, and it seemed to tremble. There was no one in or around it she could see, though! *How?*

Forgetting about her shoe entirely, curiosity took Aiella over, and she stood up, doing her best to stay hidden still but trying to see if anyone was inside the vehicle. It looked empty, so she took this opportunity to get a closer look. She could not see any sign of movement as she thought she had seen from further away. Aside from the noise it was making, it otherwise looked like the vehicle was standing still, not so much as vibrating. As she ran closer, she kept crouched low in case someone were to appear - not that anyone should. Her mind was whirring with questions, and then the sound suddenly stopped. She froze, looking only with her eyes for any sign of motion. There was none.

"Thank goodness," she whispered. Running closer, she ran her fingers along the exterior of the truck, exhilarated by the mix of rusty and smooth edges. She thought to herself how fun it must have been to grow up with machinery such as this, hopping in the back of the truck, laughing with friends. *Friends.* If only Luke and Alexis could see this. Or Frank! *Or Eli.*

Glancing inside the truck, she found no signs of life. *Odd*, she thought, *how did this get here?* She stood upright and peered in more fully, her hands trembling on the window. All she could see were strange pieces of metal, glowing slightly. They differed from anything she had ever seen before. No humans or living monsters were in there, at least.

She circled the body of the vehicle. The back was a lot roomier than she had noticed inside the books she read, deceptively so in fact. She stared at the back window with the bed of the truck in front of her, an urge to play pretend more persistent than she could hold back.

It was impossible to resist, and she hoisted herself up onto her arms and threw her legs over the back of the giant machine and onto the bed, scooting herself against the side. How wonderful to imagine her loved ones beside her, telling a funny story and holding hands. Happy.

In her mind, they were always all happy.

But a sudden jolt made her clutch her arms against the inside of the walls and widen her eyes.

The noise. It was back again.

She quickly forced her vision in through the window as the engine purred louder and forced the vehicle forward. *How is this moving?!* There was still no sign of a single person inside the cab, and that terrified her more than anything. She ducked down against the back of the truck, being sure to keep her head below the window in case someone was about to pop out. She found herself not breathing, her hands turning white from squeezing what she could below her so hard. The hope she had of finding answers about The Elder quickly diminished. She stared straight ahead, watching the destroyed downtown area become smaller and smaller as the truck gained speed.

Chapter 6

Aiella shook her head to refresh her thoughts. *Breathe*, she warned herself. *Stay calm. Just breathe.* She considered trying to jump over the side and escape the moving vehicle, certain it would leave her safer than staying. However, as she scooted to the side and dared to look over the edge, she immediately felt dizzy. Panic set in. This was going faster than she had ever known possible before! *I'm going to die. I'm going to die.* She lay down in the fetal position and closed her eyes. Any chance of jumping off and running back home was already past. *Please don't let me die.* She squinted her eyes shut, counting her inhales and exhales, counting to high numbers, picturing herself in the mountains, anything to slow her rapid heart rate. Nothing worked.

The road bumped below the truck, making Aiella more ill. *You're okay,* she tried to remind herself. But no matter how much effort she used to convince herself, she sweated with chills, her breath becoming shorter and shorter, her chest in knots. After some chunk of time had passed, she finally sat back up from lying in the bed, the cool breeze helping to soothe her stomach. The sun was setting beside her, meaning they were heading south. She forced herself to look inside the truck again now that the light was fading and shook her head in disbelief, trembling.

She had been correct in her assumption that no person was inside the truck driving it. It was not merely driving itself, though, either, as she finally had conceded in her thinking. Instead, she realized that the chunks of metal she had seen earlier were in fact androids or robots of sorts, fueled by a small flame on their underside. She sighed a breath of relief, happy they likely would not wreck them. Their programming wouldn't allow that. *Right?* Frank had told her about little metal friends such as these that had become more common before the outbreak. *It's normal.*

Aiella only hoped they would arrive wherever they were going soon so she could hide and begin the long trek home. The further they drove, the longer her journey back to her loved ones would be. She stifled a sudden urge to sob, knowing that if she stayed gone for too long, her family would find it more difficult to survive on the rations she left. Worse, they might leave the tunnel and catch the disease she still was not sure had been eradicated. *So much for helping them,* she thought, shaking.

They turned towards the sun that was now almost all the way down, Aiella cursing that now she could not see where they were. She tried her best to feel whether their speed was staying consistent or slowing down, but it felt like they were going faster still. Trapped. Lying back in defeat, with a tear streaking down her face. She closed her eyes, thinking about bits and pieces of a conversation with Luke and Alexis. She wished they were with her now.

"2113 was the year that the outbreak started, as you two know," she started sinisterly. *They nodded in agreement, eager for what she was going to tell them. It reminded her of how excited small children behave. "Before the outbreak, there were buildings, shiny buildings, made mostly of glass, that went hundreds of feet up into the sky. Streets were paved a slick black and were covered with thousands of people at a time. Some walking, some in cars, some on hoverboards, and others still in their new, and very limited, hovercraft vehicles." They looked at her in awe; the twinkle of the lantern added a sparkle to their faces that forced happiness.*

"I'm not sure if I ever saw a hovercraft, but I am sure I would have loved it. Few people had the privilege of owning them since they had just finally reached the market before the outbreak happened. Cars on the ground were too congested, so the natural next step was to get off the streets. Hovercraft vehicles that were released had ads for soaring high over buildings, but that is not what actually came out. Not yet, anyway. The first ones, the only ones that ever got put to market, could only fly about ten feet off the ground, and had to be over the streets still. It was just enough to go over cars and the drones that acted as stoplights. When the outbreak happened, they were the first things to disappear. It made it so much easier for the select few who owned them to escape elsewhere." She stopped for a moment, wondering how she had gotten away from the region, and pondering the idea that maybe she had been in a hovercraft-type vehicle before.

"Someday," she had promised. "Someday, we will all get to leave this den and live a normal life. A beautiful one surrounded by fresh air and nature." Alexis and Luke smiled at her, and she thought she saw in the light's glow a slight brush of each other's hands.

Aiella opened her eyes again, staring up at the darkening sky. It was the last bit of their conversation that she couldn't escape from now, no matter how hard she tried. Would that be a promise she kept?

Considering how strange this truck was to be on, she couldn't imagine being in a vehicle that flew. It didn't seem natural. If they ever could live a normal life, she hoped it could be primitive. Surrounded by and being one with nature, no crazy machinery or slick black roads paving through the environment. Closing her eyes again, she calmed her body by giving it only thoughts of building treehouses in the forest; the wind whipping playfully at those she loved most.

Eventually, the sky seemed to brighten over Aiella's eyelashes again. Her head immediately jerked up when the truck came to a sudden stop, her entire being acutely aware of her surroundings, instinct taking over. She heard clanking, like metal falling over onto itself in their kitchen. If these robots had been programmed, then by whom? An icy chill ran down her spine at all the possibilities. Aiella grabbed every ounce of energy and courage she could muster and dragged herself up to view what was on the other side of the truck.

Directly overhead, several tall metal structures gave off a yellowish glow, projecting onto the roads below. Although it was dark, she couldn't make out any stars. Looking around her, it seemed she was in an alley of some sort - or at least she thought that's what it was called. Giant brick buildings similar to those from Old Spokane were shooting towards the sky on either side of the truck, only a few feet away in both directions. Trash and old cans lined the dirty ground. Aiella was unsure whether it was paved. She crawled low to the back of the truck bed, peeking over toward the end of the narrow road she was on.

While another building blocked the direction the truck was facing, the tail end pointed to the way out. As she rose higher from the truck bed, gripping the cold metal with all her might, she gasped, ducking back down. Much to her astonishment, she wasn't just in a small town or some random standalone building. She was in a large city. A *well-lit* city. With towers soaring higher than she had ever known possible. If there were lights, and trucks, and litter that looked recent, that meant...

There were others.

"Well, goodnight then," a voice boomed. She ducked in fear. But no one was speaking to her directly. *Was that another human?*

"Goodnight," a voice said back. With just enough emotion behind it, she could confirm her initial thoughts: there were people here.

Aiella's heart raced as she searched within herself for answers telling her what to do. She didn't know where she was, did not know how to drive a truck, and also didn't know how to move from the position she was in without being seen. She thought she might hyperventilate to death, and wished so badly that Frank, Eli, or literally anyone she knew was here. Surely they would know what to do. Right?

She swallowed nervously, knowing only she could save herself. If she had put herself in this position, she would find a way out. She had to. For the sake of her family.

A painful twinge crept through her, regretting not telling Frank she was going to look for answers to the peculiar questions revolving around her.

When she didn't hear any voices for a consecutive thirty seconds, she hopped over the side of the truck and quickly hid behind one of the large tires. Thankfully, there was no one behind her on what looked like a one-way street backing up against a crooked building, and she was thankful she looked to have gotten out of the vehicle undetected. She peered around the tire, looking at the bright lights at the end of the alley, squinting her eyes. When she saw no movement, she crept alongside the wall nearer to it, being sure to stay crouched down as much as possible.

Aiella ran over thoughts of what she could say if she ran into someone over and over in her mind, ranging from questions about existence to statements of blame, not sure where to land with the conversation. Who were these people? Where was she? Who did the small machines belong to? How was the truck running if they hadn't stopped for a recharge? Why had none of them found her or the others before and welcomed them here? Did she want to be found? A million different things were not adding up, including the flames. Looking around her, flames seemed to be an emblem everywhere. Bracing herself against the wall for more support, she tiptoed sideways toward the edge of the alleyway, her feet shaking like an earthquake beneath her.

As she was about to peek her head around the corner of the alley, another voice caught her, and she threw her body against the brick wall, frozen. Slipping into the shadows, the strange lights helped to create an atmosphere to hide in.

"You know what this has cost me!" The voice shouted, causing the hairs on the back of Aiella's neck to prickle. It shouldn't have, but the voice sounded vaguely familiar. She dared not breathe for fear they would find her. This man did not sound like someone you wanted to piss off or surprise, regardless of the familiarity of it.

"I-I'm sorry, M-Master Hay-Haydn." Aiella shuddered at the obvious fear this Master was placing in his colleagues. She chewed her bottom lip until it drew blood, terrified at what he would think of someone he didn't share responsibility with. She had to get out of there, even if she had to wait it out for a while. Aiella would wait in the truck until it hopefully left back towards her home, and that was final. She hadn't seen the droids or robots, or whatever they were, bringing anything back with them, so she strongly felt a return trip would be necessary.

Confident in her decision, she began scooting back into the far depths of the alley.

POP!

Aiella jumped, causing way too much noise as she realized she had stepped on an old cup and shattered it. Thinking fast, she swiftly dropped herself low to the ground, coming face to face with a dead rat. Struggling not to gag, she held her breath, straining her neck sideways to see if anyone had heard.

"What was that?" The man called Master Haydn demanded.

"I'm not sure..." the other responded wearily. The Master gave a gruff snort.

"Come," his voice boomed again. "We must get to the city center for the execution."

When the figures disappeared, Aiella finally let out her breath, relaxing towards the ground more fully before realizing how grotesque it was and jumping to her feet. *Execution?* She pondered, wiping her hands over her pants as she walked the rest of the distance to the truck, preparing to climb back in. She turned around towards the city, bustling with life, however eerie. Would she get the chance to see an actual lit-up city in use again?

Likely not. Besides, the tiny metal truck drivers had just arrived home after a long day. Surely they wouldn't be leaving again soon... if ever.

Her stomach growled as if to instruct her to go find food. To her dismay, looking in the truck, she realized she didn't have her supplies. In fact, besides the clothes she was wearing, she had nothing. She had left them in the storefront. Her stomach sank. There was no way she could attempt to return home without any supplies for herself. Her mouth ran dry, her chapped lips coarse as she ran her tongue over them. She needed water, and she needed to eat.

She had to explore this mysterious fallen city.

Chapter 7

Stepping cautiously out of the alley, the orange glow of the lights every which way blinded Aiella. Blinking rapidly to adjust, she saw banners of a middle-aged man rippling carefully in the slight breeze. THANK YOU FOR SAVING US, one banner read. Another, more vibrant edition stated: OUR HERO.

Hero?

With a new, hopeful pep in her step, Aiella scanned the streets. Maybe this heroic figure could help her. Where she currently seemed to be was on the edge of a large cityscape, with buildings becoming shinier and closer together further off in the distance. Muted in the background of the buildings, the earth sloped up into a mountainside, a few faint lights showing the outline of the massive formation. Finally, it was something she felt comfortable with.

To her right, the lights gradually dimmed until they disappeared altogether, a shimmering road gently flowing down behind what looked like torn pieces of canvas, like what the curtains of the tunnels formed from.

Most astoundingly, there were people.

Actual living human beings.

Not very many people. Especially considering how large these buildings were before her. But other people nonetheless!

Each that passed had some kind of cloth bandage wrapped tightly and entirely around their face, leaving only their eyes and lips visible. To her shock, their bodies were frail. Scarred. Battered and weak. Some had lesions all the way up their exposed arms, while others walked with a limp. How could people living in the real world be more fragile than her tribe underground?

Stepping back into the shielding dark of the alleyway for another moment, Aiella quickly took off the shirt that formed her third layer, squeezing it between her legs while she took off her second layer as well. Replacing her thick top sweater over her body between shivers, she placed the other, thinner shirt between her foot and the brick wall. Pulling with all her strength, it ripped at the seams. *Perfect,* she thought with an accomplished smile. Once her face had the material tightly wrapped around it, she tied it off and tucked the remaining material underneath her tops and stepped back out of the secluded alley.

Her first instinct was to go to the right, towards the darkness. Her more natural setting. But the artificial streetlights were mesmerizing. The buzzing noise they emitted, the odd sunset color they cast... It was breathtaking, if in a sinister way. *The darkness can wait.* Her palms moistened and her heart pounded as she stepped out and strolled the city streets among strangers.

She thought she would stand out being partially barefoot, but to her surprise, most of the people she passed were without shoes. In fact, even their clothing matched hers: torn and thin and not entirely clean. Maybe this life wasn't too different from the one she was living, after all. Peeking down sideroads as she walked by them, one caught her attention. It was lit up more than the others, with a large crowd of people far off in the distance. She jumped, sparks flying overhead between them. Loud cheers followed.

The closer she walked, the more deafening the yelling became. As she drew nearer, her stomach dropped.

She had found the execution.

"Who is ready to see a criminal burn?" A voice that sounded like Master Haydn's roared. The crowd clapped and hooted. Aiella's stomach twisted even more. *Why would anyone want to watch someone die?* Still, she inched towards the crowd, ducking here and there, opening her mouth to feign chants, attempting to blend in.

"You're a monster!" The older woman on the stage spat at him. To her horror, Aiella realized the man on all the banners had been Master Haydn himself, his smug face grinning the same wretched smirk it was throughout the city. There was no way this man was a hero.

Heroes didn't kill people for pleasure.

"She thinks I'm a monster!" Master Haydn shouted to the crowd, all of whom began laughing, as if on cue.

"Maybe you shouldn't have stolen food!" someone yelled out from the sea of people. A sick grin spread across Master Haydn's face as he bent down by the woman.

"Hear that?" He told her, loud enough for everyone to hear. "Maybe you shouldn't have taken what wasn't yours, Aggie."

"You took all that wasn't yours," she retorted. "Including us."

Anger lit up *Master* Haydn's eyes, and a loud crack filled the air, forcing Aiella to bend over and cover her ears. When she looked up, the old woman called Aggie was engulfed in fire, clawing at her body as the heat licked through her skin. The smell was horrendous; the suffering even worse. And these *monsters* were watching, completely entranced as they hollered and hurrahed.

Aiella stumbled backwards, covering her mouth with one hand and her eyes with the other. A hand grabbed her shoulder fiercely, and she yelped, tripping on herself and falling to the ground. Before she turned to scurry away, she took a glance at her hooded perpetrator and gasped.

"Elder?" She panted in disbelief.

"Shhh, child." The Elder grabbed her hand and pulled her back to her feet, looking around them fervently.

"Is it really you?" Aiella murmured, gaping with wide eyes. *She had done it. She found her!* Her heart rate relaxed. Everything would be okay now.

"There's no time for chatting right now," she blurted. "Come. We have to get you home. It isn't safe here." She tugged on her arm, leading her away from the violence-hungry crowd.

"I'm so happy I found you," Aiella whispered. "We all thought you were dead."

"It would take more than a little backpacking to get your grandmother down," The Elder said with a chuckle.

Grandmother?

They walked briskly and silently down alley after alley. The Elder glanced behind them every few seconds; her face hidden by the shadow of her cloak as she dragged Aiella forward by the wrist. The center of the city may have been stunning, albeit sinister, but where she was taking her now became increasingly lackluster, pungent odors shoving themselves deep into her nostrils. Banners that had been dancing gracefully in the wind of Master Haydn even seemed dimmer the further they walked. Some were torn in half; others had small holes in them.

"Wait! You're my grandmother?" Aiella said again, this time with urgency. She had been asking the same question for the last several minutes now, greeted by a hiss and shhh every time. The Elder stopped abruptly, spinning around to face her, her nose only inches from her own.

"For the last time, child. We have to get you somewhere safe. There will be time for questions shortly." Aiella pulled back slightly, nodding. The Elder had always been quiet and reserved. She hardly spoke to anyone back at home. Now... Well, Aiella wasn't sure how much she even knew her, regardless of being related by blood. The thought sent chills running down her spine.

"But yes. Your grandmother," The Elder murmured before turning back around. "Let's go. We are almost there."

"Where?" Aiella asked, but more silence greeted her. She groaned, continuing to keep a lookout around them as they dashed through the outskirts of the city. At least they were getting far away from all those brutes at the execution. She tugged on the wrist of her sleeve, happy her face was wrapped like a mummy as tears rolled out of her eyes. Her brain now permanently held the screams of that poor woman.

Finally, they came upon the spot that The Elder—her grandmother—must have been running towards. A small cluster of thin pines stood in front of them, their branches opening into a secluded enclosure, no bigger than five to ten paces in any direction, as they ducked their heads, replacing the foul smells of this region of the city with a fresh aroma Aiella was more akin to.

"Sit. You've just seen a lot," her grandmother told her, releasing the firm grip on her arm with a sympathetic smile. She walked over to the corner and grabbed a large jug of water and a bundle of berries, gently tossing them in Aiella's direction. There were no lights, but the moon was bright enough to illuminate their faces through the trees. Aiella sat down, running her fingers over the ground.

"Moss," she said with a smile as warmth coursed through her. "That's a nice, familiar touch."

"I don't think I noticed it was there before," her grandmother replied, raising an eyebrow. Aiella unwrapped the tattered shirt from around her face and laid down, spreading out her arms as she breathed in the scent of fresh earth. She turned her head up to the openings in the miniature forest.

"Why can't we see the stars here?" She wondered, popping some huckleberries in her mouth. They had been picked far too early, the tartness making her squint her eyes as she forced another down.

"Too much light from the city, sadly."

"Did people before the outbreak never get to see the stars, then?" She asked with a frown, sitting up. Aiella couldn't imagine being free on this beautiful planet without being able to fully enjoy all its wonders. Her fingers on one hand absentmindedly found the stem of a small blade of grass, twirling it back and forth. Her other hand helped her guide water to her mouth, guzzling it as she realized how extreme her thirst was.

"To be honest, I don't know. I imagine some didn't. I have always seen the stars... and used them like a map. Before going underground, of course," she added.

"Did you used to live over here? By the city? Is that why you came here?" Aiella wiped her face on her sleeve as she bounced onto her feet, pacing back and forth as all the questions she had been keeping cooped up begged her to let them out.

"Not exactly," The Elder replied, leaning against a tree. "We aren't from this area. Volcry."

"Volcry?"

"This city," she told her. "It used to be Port Dalles, head of the Northwest Sector after the late civil war. Just before the outbreak. Now that Haydn has been ruling the area, they have renamed it Volcry." Aiella nodded her head in consideration.

"Why did you come here, then?" She inquired.

"I might ask you the same question," The Elder responded. As soon as she spoke, she suddenly kicked herself off the tree, bounding to the other side of the opening with her gaze fixed on something. Aiella walked over as well, peering with narrowed eyes as her grandmother snatched a piece of parchment out of the moonlight.

"What is that?" Aiella urged. "How did that get here?" She spun around, searching for signs of other people nearby. There were none.

"You need to leave," her grandmother spoke with widened eyes, tearing the paper up into tiny pieces before placing it in her pocket. "Now. You need to get out of here now." She made a quick round of the circular enclosure, peeking through the narrow trees into the night surrounding them. She stopped. Aiella followed her stare. Lanterns swung in the distance, their glow rapidly becoming bigger.

Someone was coming.

"Get out of here, Ella. You must go!" The Elder exclaimed, with a pained expression on her face. "This is a mess. You were never supposed to come here. This wasn't part of the plan," she said.

"What plan?" Aiella insisted. Too much was happening too fast.

"There is much more at play than you realize," she replied with a croak. "It isn't safe here. Not for anyone, but especially not for you. Since I have arrived, there have been executions three times a day. Sunrise, high sun, and sunset. If he finds you, I fear you will become the next victim." She grabbed Aiella by the wrist, jerking her to the edge of the trees, away from the lanterns.

"Look," she said, pointing a finger into the darkness. "If you look carefully, there is an entrance to the city there." Aiella strained her eyes as much as she could, but it was pitch black as far as she could see. "If you follow that path straight, at one spot beyond the alleyway, there is a brick wall with arrows all over it, pointing in every which way. When you see that, go down the road to the left of it. Stay out of sight and hurry. That pathway should lead you to the other side of the city and toward home. There's a bridge near there. Cross it. It's a long journey ahead, but you can make it."

"I'm not leaving without you." Aiella shook her head, quivering.

"You must," her grandmother pleaded. "He knows you're here, Ella. Get away before it's too late."

"Come with me, then," Aiella begged. The stubborn old lady shook her head rapidly.

"There is something I must retrieve first. The reason I came." She wrapped Aiella in a loving embrace, kissing the top of her head softly. "Your mother was my baby girl," she whispered. "I promised I would let nothing happen to you. You're all I have left, my granddaughter. Please go."

"What will you do?" Aiella asked, her chest and eyes burning.

"Give them another trail to follow." Aiella swallowed, nodding her head slowly.

"Child, GO."

Her grandmother gave her a gentle push into the trees, then rushed away in the other direction.

Chapter 8

Aiella's mouth ran dry, her heart rate picking up. Her legs felt rooted to the spot, the world around her seeming to tremble as much as she did.

She had known her grandmother all this time.

The Elder was her grandmother.

She had lived in the same tunnels with her for as long as she could remember. She was her mother's mom! And she had just found her.

Then lost her.

Shivers coursed through her as the trees whistled, cracking sounds, their needles greeting one another. She winced, shouts coming from where her grandmother had just fled. She had to leave.

Bursting out of the safety of the pine enclosure, Aiella took off running as fast as she could towards the entrance to the city her grandmother had pointed out. *Follow that path straight to the brick wall with arrows all over it. Down the road left of it. Out of the city and towards home. There's a bridge not far from there. Cross it.* The wind licked at her, trapping her hair all around her face.

Her face! It was exposed. She wouldn't blend in. She paused, glancing back from where she had left. The glow of the lights was on the branches. She couldn't go back, couldn't stop. She sprinted the rest of the distance to the alleyway.

Adrenaline rushed through her. With her blood coursing through her veins, she clawed her hair out of her face and patted it down around her back, tucking it into her shirts. It wouldn't hold for long, but at least she could see where she was going. Panting, she looked down the darkened passageway. A single small light hung on each brick building, barely casting enough luminance down for her to see the ground. She walked slowly, glancing behind her every so often, her footsteps silent and her breathing shaky. Up ahead, she could hear the drip of water, similar to what the irrigation at home sounded like every time she was heading to leave. Her stomach churned, longing to be back in her bed right now. A small mouse scurried across the ground in front of her, forcing her breath to hitch as it disappeared.

"It's just a mouse," she whispered to herself, cautiously stepping forward again. How did her grandmother know about this route? Before she could dwell on it too long, though, something jerked her to the side.

She shrieked, twirling around to find Master Haydn and one of his associates looking right at her. Aiella's mind spun with what she should do, or whether she should say anything. She had just watched this man ruthlessly execute someone over a stolen piece of food. From what she knew, he was very much human, very much alive, and dreadfully powerful. His eyes seemed to glow red, staring at her, like flames kissed his irises.

His associate looked quite different from him, though. Frail. Like the others. Aiella could see her long locks of hair matted down at the top, and the lengths were uneven. Her eyes sank into her head, and even in the limited light of the alleyway, Aiella thought she could see open wounds all over the young woman, as well as plenty of deep scars. Was this why they usually bandaged their faces? Stumbling backward, she tripped on something as it squeaked, falling onto her back with a hoarse scream.

"Who are you?" Haydn barked, clearly taken aback. He reached out a hand to help Aiella up, and she momentarily felt the icy feeling of dread leaving her. There was no reason for him to act like a monster towards her.

"E-E-Ella, sir," she stuttered, a blend of emotions and cold air around her. Something smelled like it was rotting. The dread quickly started creeping back into her. Grabbing his hand to allow him to pull her to her feet, a blazing sting burned through her arm.

"You." Master Haydn growled. Her face glistened with sweat as he turned towards the roads behind them. "Guards!"

"Guards? What? No!" Aiella shrieked. "I am not dangerous! I didn't mean to come here; I just want to go home!" With a grunt, two large men, who resembled the woman in appearance, came into sight, and she felt tears threatening to roll down her face.

"This one." Master Haydn gestured toward Aiella. "Take her."

"No!" she protested, the horrible smell growing stronger as they took a few long strides to reach her. She wanted to beg, to run, to explain everything, but she bit her tongue, realizing with horror that these people showed all the awful first signs of the ceremotosis. The scars were singe marks. The smell of burning flesh. This had to be another one of her nightmares. *Wake up, Ella! Wake up!* She pleaded, trying to reach to pinch herself.

"Well, well," Master Haydn said with menace. "It seems grand old Athena did exactly what I thought she would to save you." He cackled, the sound making Aiella turn pale.

"Who is Athena?" She spoke out. Guards grabbed her arms from behind, shackling them together painfully.

Master Haydn let out a chortle. "Why, your little grand-mom, of course!"

"What did you do to her?" She demanded through gritted teeth, pulling away from the guards. It was to no avail. "Why do you know her?" She yelled, attempting harder to wither herself free.

"Nothing... yet," he said with a grin. "I was too busy coming to find you." He gave a nod to the guards, and Aiella felt a hard object hit the back of her head before falling unconscious.

Chapter 9

The following hours played in flashes of bits and pieces of information in Aiella's mind, interrupted frequently by sudden darkness and harsh voices. The disease was everywhere, just like in her nightmares.

She had no way of judging how much time had passed when she could finally open her eyes for more than a split second. No light was available when she did. She felt all around her; her whereabouts seemed akin to the tunneled home she missed desperately right now, but she knew it was not. Was she blind? Had all that artificial light made her lose her vision?

She placed her hand on the back of her head, keenly aware of how much it was throbbing. Dehydration crept into her again, and worry was settling in faster than she could try to reason it out. Aiella sat up straight, hearing a jingling noise to her right. Scooting back, she found herself up against a wall. Her eyes were adjusting now, and she saw that there was a small sliver of light coming in from above her, where she had heard the noise. *A pit?* Sure enough, she looked around again and saw that she was indeed inside a little rectangular pit. Feeling behind her, her hands curved with the familiar rocks and dirt that made the tunnels at home. The familiarity gave her hope. She imagined she was there now, taking deep breaths to gather her senses.

Up ahead, at the top of the drop, a door shone light in from beneath it. From what Aiella could make out in the limited luminance it gave, there was just enough of a platform jutting out over her near the door for people to open it without immediately falling in. She couldn't help but wonder how the captors got her in here. Though it was dark, she guessed the door was easily six to eight feet off the ground. She stood up, walked over underneath the platform, and tried to jump up to reach it. No luck. Her captors obviously dropped her down into this pit cell. *Guess that explains the headache.*

Aiella sighed, walking to the wall next to the door and looking up at it wistfully. She touched her head again, speculating if they had just thrown her down here like a dead animal. She shuddered. If the door was unlocked, she deliberated that there had to be a way to climb out. *That wouldn't be a very sophisticated prison system, though,* she argued with herself. Surely they secured it from the outside. Oddly, she still felt more at peace here than in the streets. The dusty air and lack of light were something she was used to. She sat down to think, only to realize how much physical trauma her body had experienced in the last couple of days. Her foot from when she left her shoe in the shop in Old Spokane was throbbing, and her makeshift bandage was torn to pieces. Her head pounded, her heart was beating out of her chest, and both her wrists and shoulders were in steady pain from being grabbed and forced together so harshly. Wriggling her hands in front of her, she realized they had removed her cuffs.

Aiella winced, emotional angst more painful than that of her exhaustion and wounds. She missed everyone she knew, churning uncomfortably with hunger and thirst. *How long was I unconscious?* She would surely die here if she didn't get out soon. But if she was going to plan an escape, she was cognizant of the fact that she needed to be at least a little more rested.

Though she knew more people surrounded her than she knew existed just twenty-four hours before, she felt more alone than ever as she curled up on the dirty floor and tucked her eyes and thoughts away, letting herself succumb to her weakness.

Aiella woke up to the sound of a fist on the door above her, her dreams fading as she realized again that this was not another nightmare she could wake herself up from. She scurried over to the corner, holding her knees tight against her chest. Breath suspended in the air like a snowflake, she waited for the intruder behind the door to say something. Instead, he opened it, his silhouette dark and foreboding against the bright background. Forcing her eyes to adjust to the light, Aiella looked up behind the guard for any clue where she was being held prisoner. She still didn't know what else was at play to deserve this title or treatment.

Behind the large body, she could immediately tell she was outside. Or rather, the door leading out to the world was outside, and it was afternoon or evening. She wondered yet again how long she had been down there. It seemed there were large cylindrical columns not too far away, reminiscent of the outdoor courtyards of castles she had seen in fairytales. To think, a couple of days ago, she had been feeling hopeless and trapped at home, sure that no one else could exist or help. Now, here she was, taken prisoner by burned individuals who had a beautiful fortress and threw her into a pit underground. She clutched her head in dizziness, resulting in her looking away from the doorway just as he threw something down at her.

"Eat," the shadow said.

"What if I am not hungry?" She asked in defiance, not wanting him to leave, and shut that door again, locking her alone in the dark.

"You are." He sounded so confident. "Your questioning will be in three hours."

She stared at him and said nothing.

After a long pause, he spoke again. "You really should eat," he said, this time more tenderly, the hint of a pity-filled smile behind his voice making her wonder if her eyes and ears were deceiving her. Why would this stranger keeping her trapped down here have any reason to show her a shred of kindness? When she still didn't respond, he shook his head with a shrug and shut the door again.

"Wait!" Aiella cried, but to no avail. It didn't matter; he was already long gone, blackness enclosing her once again.

She blindly crawled over cautiously toward where he had thrown food down to her, curious what he could have possibly given her to eat, and why. It could easily be a trap, or laced with poison, but her stomach was aching so badly from hunger that she didn't care. It was a risk she had to take. Finally, in the middle of the room, she felt a lump that hadn't been there before. She tried to force her eyes to adjust to the sudden loss of light again and thought she saw the outline of a lump of bread. Next to it was a canister of sorts. She grabbed it and shook it, and to her parched delight, there was a noise of liquid inside of it. She fumbled as quickly as she could to open it, pressing it against her lips and guzzling what tasted like water. When she finished, her body longed for more, so her instincts took over, and grabbed the bread-shaped food in front of her. She had not eaten real bread before. *Here goes nothing,* she thought, bringing her hand to her mouth, and taking a bite.

It was soft and gooey on the inside, with a hard outer crust. She did not know if it was bread or not, but whatever it was, it was delicious. Finding ingredients for any type of baking was near impossible when she scavenged a few times each month, their location never changing. Having anything this dense was rare and amazing. It took very little before her stomach was full, and her soul oddly satisfied. She tucked the rest of it into her side and crawled back to the edge of the room, watching the doorway, and nibbling little pieces of food sporadically.

Not long after she finished her food, the door opened abruptly with the same guard looking behind him. He jumped inside. The door swung shut quickly behind him, but caught on something that enabled just enough light to enter that they could still see each other.

The young man before Aiella looked like he wasn't more than a couple of years older than she was, with small scars on his arms, but nowhere near as bad as the rest of the people she had seen here had. Looking closer, they didn't seem to be from the same affliction, either, but like something sharp had attacked him.

"What are you doing...?" she asked cautiously, backing herself up against the wall more.

The guard chuckled softly. "We have captured you after claiming you're innocent, and that's the first thing you ask?"

"How many days have I been in the city?" She tried again, her leg muscles weak as she stayed crouched and ready to pounce or run if needed.

"Two," he replied plainly. "Which is why I said you needed to eat and drink. Which," he said, looking around them, "it appears you have." He turned back to her, raising an eyebrow.

"My birthday..." Aiella mumbled under her breath.

"Come again?"

"Today is my 18th birthday," she repeated quietly. "Not that you care."

The guard widened his eyes, visibly swallowing. Aiella glanced up nervously at the ceiling of the pit. Slowly, she moved her head back down to look at the man before her. Their eyes locked, catching her breath in her chest as her heart started pounding. Though it was still somewhat dark, his eyes were glowing the brightest gold color, lessening her fear. She didn't want to keep staring at him, but a warmth unlike any other she had felt before filled her entire being to a point where she couldn't help it.

"You told me to wait when I was leaving before," the guard told her, not tearing his eyes away from her. "I... Could I come sit closer?" He gestured to the spot beside her on the wall. Still looking directly at him, Aiella nodded slowly. *Who is this guy?*

"Happy birthday," her foreboding captor whispered. "I'm sorry you have to enjoy it from down here. You deserve so much more."

Aiella shook her head, forcing herself to stop staring at the stranger. "You don't know me or what I deserve," she told him.

"I know more than you think," he responded, looking up at the door he had jumped through. How had he bounded down to her from that height without hurting himself? Before she could question it, he cut off her thoughts. "Aiella, right? Don't tell that to Haydn during questioning." *How does he know my full name?*

"Who are you?" Aiella demanded.

"My name is Zale," the guard told her softly. "I'm not from here, much like yourself."

"Where are you from?" She questioned. Zale simply shook his head.

"Does Master Hadyn man know you are down here with me?" She asked. Again, he shook his head. *"Ah, a rebel."*

"You'd probably starve to death if it were up to Haydn," Zale told her nonchalantly. Aiella shivered. "Are you cold?" Zale asked, a concerned look creeping its way onto his tan face.

"A little," she admitted, "although more confused than anything. Why would a man I have never met want me to starve? Why am I down here?" Hot water started streaming down her face uncontrollably.

"Shhh, it's all right. It will be okay," Zale soothed, scooting over and placing an arm over her shoulder. When she didn't pull away, he wrapped his other arm loosely around her in a hug. She never imagined she would cry in the arms of a stranger on her eighteenth birthday, but here she was, being weirdly comforted by someone helping to hold her prisoner.

Aiella pulled back awkwardly, turning to wipe her face on her arm. "I'm sorry," she muttered.

"Don't be," he told her. "I'm more sorry than anything." With his tone, Aiella really thought he meant it. His eyes glanced down at her feet. "You cut your foot." Aiella wasn't sure if it was a question or a statement of the obvious.

"Yes," she breathed. Now that attention was on it again, it throbbed more painfully.

"That doesn't look good," he told her with concern. "I need to clean that."

"Oh no. You don't need to, I'm sure it's fi—"

Zale cut her off, gently touching the area surrounding the wound.

"Ow!" she cried out in pain.

"Infected." He spoke matter-of-factly.

"Great," she moaned. "That's just what I need. I'm trapped in a pit for no reason, with an infection taking over my foot. I'm never going to get back home…"

"Chin up," he told her, putting a finger to her chin and lightly pulling it upwards. "I'll help you clean it. I can't dress it, though. Master Haydn would recognize the bandaging."

"There isn't any way you could get me more water, is there?" She shut her eyes in anticipation of the answer.

"Yes, of course!" Zale hopped to his feet, ready to rush off to grab more. "Although I can't come back down immediately," he said sadly. "I've been with you too long already. It will have to wait a little while." Aiella nodded her understanding. "All right then," he said, getting ready to leap. Aiella hadn't realized how tall he was before. He was not as tall as the pit, but with his arms extended all the way, the dirt overhang before the door was not too far off. She watched in awe as he crouched down and jumped, hooking his hands on the small opening that led to the ground outside.

When he returned later, Zale turned on a small blue lantern.

"Why are you helping me?" She asked him timidly. "It could kill you. I saw what happened to that woman in the city."

He gave her a solemn look. "*Aiella*, you are a nice girl. A smart girl with more influence than she knows. You do not deserve to die. I only pray you'll make it back to your family." He gave a curt nod.

"Thank you," she murmured, every minute a fresh surprise.

"Don't thank me yet," he said, lips pursed. "Let me see that foot. We have only a few minutes before I must leave again to prepare for more questioning."

Aiella grimaced as she put her foot up on a nearby crate he had brought, knowing what was coming. Zale fumbled under the door for the light with a smaller bag before coming back over with a knife, clear liquid, and bandage.

"What is that?" She asked, with only one eye brave enough to remain open.

"Medical grade scalpel, concentrated antiseptic, and antibacterial bandage." He showcased the items as he said them. "You might want to take off your shirt and bite it," he told her.

"Excuse me?"

"You have more than one layer on, right?" She supposed he was right and must have a genuine reason for his request. She slipped her top shirt off, doing as she was told.

"Okay," he said, "One. Two. Three." Aiella bit down hard on her shirt, the entirety of her body wincing. She dared to look down and saw him slicing her heel right where her wound was. She let out a scream through the material, her body telling her to pull back, her brain reminding her this was necessary.

"I know," he said apologetically, "You have something hard embedded in here. Just..." He grimaced, squeezing her foot and reaching the scalpel in at the same time. "Just need to get it out." Aiella looked through blurred vision at a large piece of glass attached to metal coming through the surface of her foot. She forced herself to breathe, relieved it was almost out. "Almost done," he told her calmly. She nodded, tears running down her face as she continued to bite down hard on her shirt. The hard object came out completely and clanked on the hard ground. Blood poured out of her, soaking the floor.

"All right, now for the fun part," he said, looking up at her. "You okay?"

She nodded, not sure how honest she was being.

"This is going to sting quite a lot, but I need that shirt of yours."

Aiella released the material from her tightened jaw and handed it to him, inhaling a deep breath.

"There is medicine inside this that also makes you stop bleeding," he explained, regarding the clear liquid. He wiped the blood from her heel before immediately pouring a generous amount of the antiseptic into her wound. Aiella screamed in pain, wishing for the briefest of moments she had chosen the infection over this. Nature's way. Not even ten seconds later, though, the bleeding had subsided, and Zale had wrapped her foot tenderly in a bandage.

"Done," he said, leaning back and looking at his accomplished work. "I can only leave the bandage briefly, and then we'll have to hide it."

"Thanks," Aiella told him shakily, pulling her leg back in, noticing her shirt drenched in blood on the floor. "I guess that shirt is done for," she said. "A bear would smell that a mile away."

"Not many bears in this city," he said with a chuckle. She knew he was trying to make her feel better, but she really just wanted to be home in the woods. A bear sounded better than all of this right now.

After a couple of minutes of silence passed, Zale begrudgingly stood up. "I'm going to need that bandage. And the shirt."

"Why the shirt?" She questioned. Not that she cared. If she were ever in the wilderness again—which she hoped she would be—an animal really would smell that a mile away.

"The only way I can think of covering up my time down here is... Dark." When she said nothing, he quietly admitted: "It's not uncommon for guards to beat the prisoners. Expected, actually. The blood on the shirt... He'll assume..."

"Okay, that's enough!" She blurted out with a shudder. That someone would purposefully inflict enough pain on someone to draw that much blood made her dizzy.

"Are you okay?" he asked. His glances towards the opening of the pit told her he needed to be gone already, though.

"Yeah. Fine," she lied. How could she be okay right now? Why did he care anyway?

"Okay..." He let out a breath before inhaling deeply, now having to pull himself upward, gesturing for her to throw the other items up to him. Something that took way too much effort. "Hey," he turned back down to face her after successfully exiting, "I'm still planning on getting you water before your questioning happens shortly." Then the pit was inky again.

Chapter 10

Zale hadn't returned with the water she had asked for. Was she really so naïve as to expect her prison guard to help her? For all she knew, he laced the antiseptic with some kind of poison, and she would be dead any minute now. It was impossible to keep track of time unless she were to sit and count, not that she had much better things to do. Regardless, some time went by, and she drowsily watched the door open for the third time that day. It was still light out behind Zale, his body focused in her view, but she wasn't sure if it was because of the sun setting or more artificial lights like she had seen within the city before her capture. She stood up, bracing herself for what was going to come, unable to prepare much since she didn't know what to expect. She hoped at the moment that Zale had brought something to drink.

He did not speak as he dropped a ladder down to her to climb. She contemplated whether now would be a good time to make a run for it, but Zale was far larger than she was, and she knew she could not get too far past him without putting at least one of them in danger. Her legs were sore and wobbly, but her body at least felt energized from her first meal in a couple of days.

"Climb up," he requested in a monotone voice that gave Aiella chills. She did as he said, relieved when she stood in the warmth of the last rays of sunlight. Afraid that he might have to bag her head, she looked around and took everything in as quickly as she could. She was right. Beautiful stone columns lined the entire walkway, which was outdoors. There was no roof above her, but to her right, there was some sort of stone building with a few beams linked to it above from the columns. The building had windows, but small, non-extravagant ones, right near the top of the wall where the roof meets the stone. It reminded her briefly of how Frank had described hospitals to be, mixed with parts he had taught her about ancient history. She considered how fortunate he would think her to be to see all of this architecture right now. The engineer in him would be giddy with delight.

Zale chuckled beside her in awe of her surroundings. "Never seen the light of day before, Ella?" he joked, looking around them before handing her a jug of water. She snatched it from him briskly, noticing the scars on his arms again.

"It's just very different here from the rest of the city that I saw," she told him flatly. Her heart started pounding as she took in the rest of him. He was quite handsome, with a robust physique. Something about him seemed... off, though. She couldn't get over the scars, looking like a knife or branch had slashed him countless times. He was still functioning, though, unlike the other scarred people she had seen. Doing a darn good job of functioning at that. Aiella ran as many scenarios as she could think of through her mind, trying to figure him out, but no answers came to her. And what about the others? The disease ceremotosis killed anyone it infected within days — anyone aside from her, at least — so she could not see how anyone else here could be alive. If, in fact, she was correct about it being the illness all of humanity feared so much. She wanted to cry again, which was unusual for her. In normal circumstances, at least. Right now, the continuing flow of questions leaking like a broken faucet into her mind overwhelmed her.

"Follow me," he told her in a low voice. Aiella was grateful to be walking again, and in the open air, taking grateful sips of water. She may not have any clue how she would get home, but at least she could relish this moment of temporary freedom. Being out in the open air gave her energy and made her feel alive. Taking a deep breath, she felt her fingers tingling, feeling as though magical abilities had taken her over. Looking beyond the columns, with the sun setting behind them, the sight was breathtaking. There was the city she had been in just days before, looming below her now. She looked all around her, trying her best to orient herself to where she was. Based on the sunset, she was walking almost directly east, and below her to the north was where the city was. She tilted her head to see as close to directly below the columns as she could, and, sure enough, it seemed to have a steep drop-off. Something was glistening below in the distance, through the trees and shining buildings. Beyond them, a line of sparkling purple and orange hues was mesmerizing. It reminded her of the creeks in the forest when just enough light was hitting them.

A river! She thought to herself excitedly, Zale watching her contentedly the whole time. She squinted her eyes; the sun dimmed more quickly than she would like and confirmed her hypothesis. It was a river, the last of the sun reflecting off its surface. This river was unlike any other she had ever seen: it was gigantic! The Pacific Northwest was full of natural elements even before the outbreak, but this was more massive and beautiful than she could imagine a body of water being. *No wonder The Elder said there was a bridge I needed to find!*

The Elder. Her grandmother.

Aiella's open-mouthed smile quickly turned to a frown. Zale gave her a simultaneously amused and confused glance, his grip accidentally tightening around her wrist. She winced, gasping out in pain.

"Sorry!" he apologized, loosening it immediately. "Habit, I suppose..."

They turned right around the corner of this peculiar castle of sorts, and the daylight left with it. Walking away from the water and city, she felt the dusky darkness crawl beneath her skin.

"Is everything all right?" Zale questioned. As if everything could be all right with her, given the situation.

"Do you know where my grandmother is? Athena, I think Haydn called her?"

Zale gave her a sad smile, shaking his head slowly.

"Is she dead?" Aiella gasped in horror, clasping her free hand to her face.

"No, no," Zale rushed to tell her, taking her other hand in his. Electricity bolted through her from her fingertips to her toes, making her quiver. "We captured her, though," he said solemnly.

The blood drained from Aiella's face, her heart being squeezed with fear for her family member, before her gaze settled on the giant doors in front of them. A torch on either side was hanging from the cool outer brick walls, cascading a foreboding orange glow onto them. A strange writing hung over the entrance, etched into the stonework.

"What does that say?" She asked Zale.

"What?" he asked, turning around to follow her gaze. She nodded her head upwards.

"Is it... Latin?"

Zale raised an impressed eyebrow at her. "You know Latin?" he queried.

"No."

"It's in an ancient language, but means *He who desires, takes all things.*" The sentiment sent shocks down her spine in the worst way. Would she ever get to see another sunset after speaking with this Master Haydn?

"Why does he want me?" She asked in a near-inaudible voice, terror-stricken at what was to come next.

"He's been looking for someone, and he thinks you are her."

"Am I?"

"That's not important." He was stern. Aiella did not pry further; the knots in her chest and stomach tightened until she was sure she would throw up.

"There is no reason he should hold me prisoner. Why am I being questioned?" She raised her voice slightly, though she quivered on the inside. "Please," she added, her voice now much quieter as two large double doors drew nearer. "Please, I just want to go home."

"I told you, he thinks you are who he has been searching for. It would do you good not to mention a home in there."

"But why has he been searching for me?" She pleaded, surprised by his hushed tone. He gave a curt shake of his head as two more guards appeared at the front of the doors to greet them.

"Ah, they have arrived!" One of them shouted behind her. The one who spoke looked dark and vile, like she could snap at any moment, her eyes red with heat. She, along with the other guards, had the same appearance akin to the ceremotosis disease, like the one that Aiella originally saw upon arriving. She was thankful they had assigned Zale as her guard. Day quickly turned to night. Though she knew Zale couldn't be on her side, at least she felt alarmingly safe near him. For all he seemed to know about her, she wondered if he had somehow been assigned to be her guard on purpose.

"Master requests her in the east wing," the other guard told Zale, he much smaller in stature than the others. Zale simply nodded, then shuffled Aiella quickly through the doors.

She knew she should be nothing but afraid right now, but seeing the inside of this building had her star-struck. If she thought the outside of this fortress was beautiful, then saying the interior was beautiful would be a gross understatement. The entire floor and ceiling were reflecting golden artificial light in every direction, and the walls were a brilliant maroon and blue pattern that made Aiella want to do nothing but curl up and sleep. *Is this guy some sort of king?* She asked herself. Fear struck through her, suddenly on high alert that this questioning could end in execution, much like many of those fairytales with kings involved, and much like the lives in this city seemed to. *Three times a day,* her grandmother had warned her.

Aiella looked around her, trying to break her concentration beyond the gorgeous glow of the floor and ceiling with that ever-comforting wall. She realized the blue and purple hues were covering only the middle part of the wall, the top and bottom portions still being that golden reflective material. There did not seem to be anywhere to go from here, feeling like you were a guest of the sun. She logically knew this could not be the case, and forced herself to look beyond the beauty, thinking that they set it up this way on purpose to be an optical illusion. Not two moments later, she unmistakably saw the outline of another door ahead, and another to their left that seemed to draw them in. *That must be the east wing,* she decided. Before she could be pulled entirely in that direction, she looked to her right, pleading for her eyes not to betray her, and for a split second, she could have sworn she saw a door, behind which there was an endless hallway of white with a plethora of windows behind it. She blinked her eyes, and it was gone, unable to be found again since the guard was tugging her in the opposite direction.

"Please don't let me die," she begged Zale quietly. "I'm not who he wants. I did nothing wrong. Please. My family." Her voice faltered, trying to meet his warm, glowing eyes again. His face denied her like a cold, hard statue.

"Play dumb," he whispered harshly. "And don't mention your family." Then, he forcefully pushed her in through the door of the east wing.

Chapter 11

Aiella stumbled into a large, bright room with two chairs inside it, the door shutting silently behind her.

"Hello!" Master Haydn grinned from atop a tall chair. The walls, ceiling, and floor were all the same, blinding shade of gray. *More optical illusions? What is this castle hiding?* Aiella blinked several times, trying to adjust. "Please sit," he continued, opening his hand towards the other chair in front of him.

Aiella walked swiftly to the chair he was pointing at and sat down, folding her hands nervously in her lap.

"You are probably wondering why you are here," he started, raising an eyebrow.

"Yes, sir. Master." She corrected herself, looking up at him and clearing her throat. "Yes, I wonder that," she said, this time more composed.

"You don't look infected with ceremotosis," he said to her. Aiella was not sure if he was saying it as a statement in her questioning, or as an observation. She merely stared back at him.

"Ah," he said, leaning back with a hand on his face, "a silent betrayer."

"What? No!" she shot back. "I am not a betrayer. I have done nothing wrong."

"And yet, here we are," he retorted with a smirk. "It's too bad that we are not on the same page." His attitude towards her was heating her, making her even more uncomfortable with the situation.

"Well, what are we to do about it, then?" She said, glaring back at him. Zale walked in at that instant with a rope.

"Just to be precautious," Master Haydn said down to her, his words dripping with a loathing that had to run deeper than a simple convict sneaking into a truck. Zale grabbed her hands and tied them loosely together behind the chair. Aiella tried to make eye contact with him before he left again, searching his face for any signs of what was going on or was going to happen, but she found nothing. Still, she felt she could trust him, and as she could move her hands and wrists enough to slip out of the hold he made, she knew she could confirm he wasn't all bad. Aiella found her antagonistic side bubbling through, turning her back to *Master Haydn*.

"Are you a king?" She asked defiantly, "Why does everyone call you *Master*?" Hatred seethed through her. Aiella was unsure of where these dark feelings were coming from. Maybe it was just from the execution, but she *loathed* him.

Haydn seemed unamused. "I think we should start the questioning, shall we?" Aiella stayed planted with the same blank face. "First question: How did you get to my kingdom?"

"Kingdom? That's bold. On a truck," she replied plainly.

"Where did you find a truck?"

"On *your* truck," she specified, "the one in the alley. Surely you could put that together on your own." She feigned an exasperated frown.

"Where did you find the truck?" He asked, his face deepening. Aiella thought smoke might bubble out of his ears at any minute. She smirked.

"In the middle of nowhere. I'm not even sure; I was lost."

"Was no one with you?" He pushed.

"I've been wandering on my own for a while," she lied. "I can't remember the last time I saw someone, actually. Until now, I thought I was the only person left alive on the entire planet." She stared at him.

"Peculiar thing... A young and *weak* girl being able to live on her own for years. Not harmed by nature, untouched by the disease..." Aiella shrugged.

"I guess we'll see if I catch it now that I've been around you all here. Big mistake on my part, really."

Haydn leaned forward in his chair, his hands clenched together. "It doesn't. Add. Up!" She flinched at his last word, vicious spit flying through the room. She kept her mouth held tightly shut.

"So, tell me!" he yelled at her in fierce demand, leaving the comfort of his chair and stepping down in one large leap to right in front of her. "Tell me," he said through gritted teeth, circling where she sat, "where have you been the past decade?"

Aiella looked at him as he circled her chair threateningly. She was unsure what to say, and frankly, suddenly too afraid to say much of anything, anyway. The surge of defiance she had felt previously was now gone, replaced by intimidation. She was ashamed that she had thought leaving home, and the comfort of her routine, was a good idea. She had found The Elder, but then lost her anyway. Her mission had failed. What would Alexis and Luke think when they eventually had to admit she was dead? Surely, she was going to die here. This man—the one who had wealth and an abundance of power—was insane. She shook her head.

No, she would not allow herself to end here.

"I was in the old city of Spokane," she said slowly, testing his reaction.

"With whom?" he shot back.

"No one," she lied again, confidence returned to her. She obviously had something he wanted, and that made her more powerful. He glowered at her. Perhaps he really had been looking for her.

"That. Isn't. POSSIBLE!" he screamed. Aiella shut her eyes, but still didn't give in. She wouldn't let him have her.

"It's true," she continued, trying to remain as calm as possible. "There are plenty of resources in that region." She *had* been the one for years that helped support her family, explained how getting away with this could not be that hard. Aiella had to protect them. She took a deep breath.

"At first it was difficult - or at least I imagine it was. Maybe I had someone tending to me when I was younger. Maybe a mama bear? For as long as I can remember, I have been a lone wolf." She paused, glancing at him to see if he had anything to say. He hissed through his crinkled expression, his face redder than before. Even his hair seemed to redden as he glared at her, waiting impatiently for her to continue.

"I taught myself how to spear fish and gather berries and other foods from the plants nearby. Used remnants from the destroyed cities to help me cook and create small weapons for self-defense. I sleep inside the buildings. I hadn't seen the truck running before, so went in for a closer look, trying to see if there was a threat to me. When I didn't see anyone, I hopped onto the back to make certain no one was there. No one was, but then the truck left, and I didn't know what to do, so I laid down, and I waited. I got off as soon as I could, and you found me in the alley."

Aiella recalled the genuine memories she was referring to. Frank had taught her how to spear a fish, as well as gather plants that were not poisonous for them to eat. He had taught her how to boil water to clear bacteria out of it, and how to create simple circuits. She knew basic engineering in terms of underground architecture and knew how the water well filtration system was built and maintained. Aiella thought that if anyone aside from her in the tribe were in her position right now, their odds of survival would be much slimmer. She did not think that arrogantly by any means, but reflecting on her life and skill set, she realized she may still have a chance in this strange place.

She thought harder about the day that Frank had taught her how to fish. *It's all about a change in perspective,* Frank had told her. It surprised her she was remembering this so vividly right now. *See the spear,* he told her. *Watch it when I stick it inside the water. Watch where it goes.* Aiella watched in wonder as it appeared to bend. Her shock must have been apparent, for Frank laughed out loud, taking the stick out and pushing it back slowly into the water again.

"Well, well," Haydn spoke, startling Aiella back to the present. She felt like she had just awoken from a trance, and it frightened her.

"Who is Frank?" Master Haydn spun around, placing his face only inches from hers and glaring at her with hatred. He knew she had lied. *How?* She thought. What did he know?

"How?" He snickered. She sat up straight, eyes wide. He was reading her mind. She tried to clear her thoughts, but it was nearly impossible. She had to wonder if he had manipulated her into thinking about those sentimental memories to begin with. Haydn nodded his head in amusement.

"You're a monster," she whispered.

"No," he said with a grin. "Just enhanced." He paused dramatically and placed a finger on his chin. "As I imagine you are, too." Aiella thought she might vomit, being compared to the likes of this... man.

"What are you talking about?" she spoke through her teeth, her mind foggy and strength dwindling as she desperately tried to stand up, realizing she would have to undo her hands first, no matter how loosely tied they may be.

"For starters, you are not diseased, and clearly never have been. You have matured more than I ever expected," he said, looking her up and down with a hunger that terrified her. "I have been around many others like you before," he continued, the hairs on her neck prickling up. "I understand your potential. Yet wonder still, how all these years I have been searching for you, I could not find you?"

Aiella shook her head vigorously. "I am not who you think I am. I am Ella, just Ella. No one special, and *certainly* not like you!" she spat.

"I could put this questioning on hold, not prosecute you any further, if you join my side. Your wretched parents should have taken me up on the same offer." His eyes lit up, making Aiella's stomach twist.

"I have nothing you want," she shouted. "I don't even know my parents, but I saw what you did to that woman!"

"You have *everything* I want," he replied harshly. "And if you think what I did to her was bad, just wait until what I have in store for you. So, *Ella*. Last chance. Join me." He stretched an arm out. She shook her head fervently.

"Never. You take innocent people and condemn them. *Kill* them. I will never join you!" She said menacingly.

"A pity, really," he said with a click of his tongue. "Your choice, though. Zale! Bring it in!" He yelled towards the door. Aiella froze, terrified of what he could bring that would further this discussion. Was this going to be the end?

A few moments passed before Zale came rushing back in, a gorgeous plant fluttering in the breeze that the door opening caused. *I'm sorry,* he mouthed to Aiella, setting the beautiful tree in front of Haydn before swiftly leaving again. *Sorry for what? It was magnificent!*

"Living in the wild, I am sure you've seen a tree before?" Haydn pushed, eyes too bright.

"Yes... This one is exceptional, though. I haven't seen one quite like it before," she told him, entranced to a point where her fear and rage diminished.

Haydn laughed deeply, an echoing sound sending chills through Aiella. "Well then," he sneered, "this should be extra pleasurable for me."

"What do you—?" The loud explosion of fire cut Aiella's question to Haydn off. "No!" she shouted instinctively, ducking her head. But he did not direct the fire at her. In an instant, the flame reached the plant, crippling Aiella.

"Stop it, stop it!" She screamed, writhing off the chair in pain, white spots covering her vision as needles of fire drove themselves through her bones. She could hear it, hear the agony, the last afflictions of the tree's last puffs before death overcame it. Aiella couldn't breathe, snakes of smoke whirling into her nose, suffocating her as Haydn bellowed in satisfaction at her torment. As the last pine needle sizzled out of existence, turbulent sobs escaped from Aiella, gasping as she struggled to take in air.

"Master!" Zale cried, "I heard a commotion. Are you all right?" Aiella stopped weeping on the floor, looked him in the eye and sensed he knew exactly what had happened. She looked at her arms, her legs, not a single mark or burn on her.

"Take her away! Her sentence is death. I have found her, and I need nothing else from her. She has chosen her fate. Her precious, insignificant life will end tomorrow." Haydn narrowed his eyes, tears boiling up in Aiella's again.

"This will be easier than I thought," Haydn said with a chuckle. "The girl doesn't even know who she is."

"Yes, Master," Zale replied. Aiella looked at him pleadingly as he jerkily grabbed her elbow and led her out. When the door closed behind them, he spoke in a hushed tone, immediately releasing his tight grip on her arm.

"He likes to pretend he did everyone a favor, you know. The planet, too. Thinking humans needed exterminating after the damage done to the natural world from the wars. But you can't fight destruction with destruction. He won't win," Zale gibbered.

Aiella was still choking and shaking, but managed out a gurgled, "What?"

Zale sighed. "No one here deserves to die, but he has the capability, and he practices it. Subjects must follow orders or risk execution. That is no way to live, and the earthlings are noticing it now. Resources only go to the elite one. The hallway," he pointed so quickly towards the white hallway as they passed that she barely recognized him completing the motion, all the while picking up pace, "I know you saw it before. It can get you out of here. I am going to help you," he spoke in a low voice and spun around to look directly at her, his face twisted with concern. Everything here seemed more sinister by the minute. "I am sorry I cannot tell you more right now," he told her with a frown.

Then, as two other guards came into view, they shoved her through a hidden door and led her down a small sloping pathway.

Chapter 12

The pit she was now in was not as dark as the other one they had held her inside, and not nearly as deep, with a torch hanging up on the wall. There was no door, but bars wrought of iron on all sides except for one. The back wall went upward for several feet, meeting with the dirty brick ceiling. She could reach the metal bars if she stood on tiptoe, but they were too close together to allow escape. She turned and massaged her painful back and side, flinching. The smell and cries of the burning tree would not leave her, and she keeled over and threw up all over the ground. Somehow, the taste of vomit was better than the thought of reliving that. Anything was better than that. She started crying, unable to control her emotions, falling to her knees, drenching herself in her own regurgitated meal.

I am going to die. She cried to herself, pulling her knees into her chest and trying to calm her breathing. Zale may think she could escape, but even if she did, she was weak and only had a faint idea of how to return home. Escaping during daylight would be warmer and much easier for her, but they would catch her in a heartbeat. It all seemed hopeless. Which left only her haunting thoughts and unanswered questions buzzing in her brain.

What had Zale meant when he said Haydn thought he was saving everyone? And the planet, too? Aiella wouldn't want anything to happen to this beautiful Earth. Especially not because of humans; there were so many ways to cohabitate alongside the planet without destroying it. Her family did that now. Did her protective instincts of nature make her like that heartless beast? The one who laughed maniacally as he watched people burn?

Her blood ran cold. Chilled sweat covered her face as it occurred to her that the fire in her interrogation had appeared from nowhere. And Haydn had *read her mind*. How was any of that possible?

She whipped her head towards the large doors that kept her contained, the silhouette of someone familiar coming into view in the flickering light of the flaming torches.

"This has to be quick," Zale whispered, unlocking the large iron cage and clambering down to her. The door ahead could not be closed.

"You," she whispered with a quiver. "You're the reason I am being executed. You knew exactly what he was going to do to me. But you only told me not to give details of my life, not to admit fully who I was. It didn't matter, and now he wants me dead. Why didn't you warn me more? Your advice didn't help; it just made it worse!" Quiet sobs threatened to break free for the millionth time that day.

Zale shook his head desperately, cupping her cheek in one of his warm hands. "You were doomed to be sentenced the minute they found you. Haydn has been searching for you for many years, and if I revealed too much and then he read your mind... Well, that wouldn't be helpful for anyone." The glow in his eyes seemed to lighten as he tenderly searched her face. Aiella thrived on his comfort, leaning into his hand more and placing her own over it.

"Who am I?" she asked Zale, looking at him with watery eyes.

"You're like me," he smiled, "and unfortunately, like Haydn. We aren't from here."

"Then where are we from? It doesn't make any sense," Aiella sniffled. "How did he read my mind? And light that tree on fire?"

"Shhh," Zale murmured, looking up in terror and shaking his head. "My allegiance is not to Haydn, and not everything you see here is what you think. It's complicated," he rushed out. "Don't you wonder how you were tortured without a single physical sign of it? Through a plant? There is a reason for all of that. Hayden knows the reason. A reason that is worth killing you for." Aiella pulled away from his hand, questions burning at the tip of her tongue.

"What is the reason?" She asked harshly.

"I can't say," Zale told her, placing a finger gently to her lips. "But I convinced him to let you see someone first. He sees it as a cruel joke, and you're both in terrible danger. But I will save you,

Ella. I promise." Then, with a bound, he disappeared as quickly as he had arrived, leaving behind a piece of bread and some water.

Who was he talking about? She hoped to see her grandmother. Hoped that she was still alive. Finding her composure, she figured she should probably devise a plan to leave. No more pitying herself. She wished she had questioned Haydn more about where she was and what had happened here. But he wouldn't have answered her, regardless. Just like everyone else. *Brute,* she thought, hating even the thought of that cruel man. What had he done to the people of this city?

She tried to think hard about everything she had viewed when she was on her walk from her first detention center to the inside of this strange castle. *The city is north straight down the mountain. On the river, I could follow it east...* Her mind trailed off, her confidence in navigating herself home stronger, but her confusion about how to escape this fortress to begin with was growing evermore. Zale had said he would help her, and she believed it. She had to. For now, she desperately needed to rest.

A few hours later, she was awakened by the clanking of metal again as it opened, and someone pushed a woman down into the shallow pit with her.

"They filled these walls with disease," the woman said. "It really is just like your mom predicted." Aiella hurled herself to the other side of the room, embracing her.

"Grandmother," she whispered with a sigh, tucking her face into her stringy hair. "Are you alright? What did they do to you? What happened after we split?"

"None of that matters now, child. I'm fine enough. We know where we ended up. We have to look towards the future from here if we want to get out alive." Aiella noticed she was walking with a limp as she circled the small den.

"Why did Haydn say there were others like me? What does he want with me?" Aiella asked, as softly as she could muster.

"It's all connected, sweetheart. You see that."

"*What* is connected?" She pushed further.

"All of it. The disease, your immunity, this city. Haydn." She waved her hand as if brushing off the subject. "We can speak of it more in depth once we get out of here. I'm just thankful you are alive." She picked up her pace, half hopping around the earthen room looking for an exit.

"Hopefully it stays that way," Aiella muttered under her breath, walking around the perimeter of the pit in the same manner that her grandmother was. Surely there had to be a way out. "He has them all enslaved, doesn't he?" she asked, pausing her search. Her grandmother took a moment to reply, starting slowly.

"Haydn thinks he saved everyone, but he did not. It would seem he stopped the progression of that damned disease for the people in this city, giving them another chance at life — or so they would think. Then yes, enslavement followed as a debt to be paid. That is all anyone has been good for to him. Enslavement to practice those damned fiery experiments while he sets out to 'do right by Earth.' Everyone will deny it, of course. He kills anyone who stands in his way. Always has..." She let out a deep breath. "Years ago, when a plague of sorts broke out here—"

"Ceremotosis?" Aiella interjected.

"Yes. That. When it broke out, everyone all over the country lost their loved ones and their lives in a matter of months. Everyone. Some were lucky enough to hide away and last longer. It all started farther east, so out here in this region, there were more lucky ones. They were more prepared. A lot of them flocked here. I watched them all drop like flies, holding you close and trying to stay as far away from Haydn as possible. It was torture, what he did to all those people," she said sadly. "Master Haydn made root during all of this and took over the Pacific Northwest Sector. Likely trying to find you by then. He came forward one day with a solution, one made from something no one had seen before. You would hear stories... Some made their way back to our little home underground, which was getting pretty settled in by then. But when someone offers a chance of survival when things look so bleak, you take it. All the citizens of Volcry took it." She stared at the wall. "He's taken and abused a lot of power in his lifetime." Aiella raised an eyebrow at her, silently begging her to finish that thought. Her grandmother merely cleared her throat and began pacing slowly again with her weak leg, continuing on a different subject.

"As soon as anyone came into contact with him, the burning would begin. Immediately, he would jump in as the 'hero,' giving them this intangible cure that stopped the progression in its tracks. Only it couldn't reverse the effects that had already taken place."

Aiella felt numb, not knowing where she fit in all of this.

"I'm still not sure I understand..." she told her grandmother, her voice trailing off.

"He started it, Ella. Haydn created ceremotosis."

The world was crumbling and falling apart.

Her family.

They were all dead because of the disease. The adoptive family she had back in the tunnels were all suffering and heartbroken at the aftermath.

And Haydn, this MONSTER, had created it.

Aiella clenched her hands; her face reddening as tears rolled quickly off her face onto the floor. The surrounding earth shook–probably another torturing session going on upstairs. Some other unfortunate soul. She would escape. She would save them all. She had to.

"Zale," she whispered hastily, taking notice there was nothing modern down here in this cell. While the city held twinkling lights and trucks could drive themselves with robots, this jail had nothing. Only dirt and pain. She wondered how many people were ushered down here to live their last moments. How many of them had been led down here by Zale? Her heart ached as it pounded harder. The warmth that filled her when she looked into his eyes, the smile that threatened to surface even in these dire situations when she saw his figure near. Aiella felt an electric shock when he touched her. She had developed feelings for him, and he was a pawn of the devil.

"Zale?" her grandmother questioned. "You've met him?"

"Yes?" Aiella said slowly, curiosity immediately calming her angry thoughts down. The surrounding shaking thankfully stopped.

"Oh, thank the Guardians," she sighed, clutching her chest with her hand. "I failed in my mission to retrieve what was needed. But perhaps not all hope is lost, my—"

"Where are you, old bat?" A deep voice yelled, interrupting her. Aiella desperately grabbed onto The Elder, clenching her ripped clothing with everything in her.

"No," she whispered fervently. "No, I won't let them take you." Her grandmother looked her in the eyes, a heavyset guard now unlocking the cell.

"Reunion is over," he said, laughed to himself as if he were the funniest man in existence.

"NO!" Aiella whimpered as she tried to stand bravely, still clinging to her last blood relative. "She did nothing!"

"It's all right, my dear child." The Elder pried her fingers off of around her, giving them a squeeze before forcing them by Aiella's side. "This has been my fate for a long time. Don't despair. Zale is from the same place as Haydn. And you," she emphasized. She leaned forward, giving her a kiss on the top of the head. "He's on our side. Trust him," she whispered, her brilliant green eyes shining with moisture.

"I love you, Grandmother," Aiella breathed, her throat constricting as heat swelled into her face.

"I know. Be safe."

Aiella swallowed, stepped back towards the wall, and sat down. Their stares lingered for a moment longer before the guard forcefully grabbed her arm and hair, dragging her towards the short ladder he had set out. If Aiella's heart had never broken before, it was crushing into a million pieces now. She winced as The Elder groaned, opening her eyes wide to see her clambering up the short ladder and away through the iron bars.

"Don't worry, princess, you will get your time to shine at sunrise," the guard said casually. Her breath hitched; her grandmother stole a look back at her one last time. Then, with a last nod from the only blood relative she had left, the guard kicked her wobbling grandmother forward, and they disappeared out of sight.

Hours later, Zale appeared at her cell again, unlocking the chamber and jumping down into her even more rushed than before.

"We only have a few minutes," he whispered urgently.

Zale tugged hard on her hand, pulling her body in close to his. Aiella trembled as the warmth from him took her over entirely, his confident arms lifting her into them. Aiella wanted nothing more than to embrace him right then and there, to forget about everything going on, to let herself find comfort... But she knew she couldn't. Time was something they had very little of. She saw he lacked a ladder, so she hoisted herself over onto his shoulders, leaning clumsily towards the doorway to climb out. She waited patiently after she pulled herself up, watching Zale leverage his body out of the ground behind her with little effort. He clutched her side immediately, looking down at a watch.

"Two minutes," he told her, pushing her ahead of him in a sprint.

It was time to break out of here.

Chapter 13

Aiella and Zale's footsteps echoed off the damp stone floors, beating a dramatic rhythm - hopefully of hope - to anyone else that may be down here. They turned upwards to the left, torches lighting the incline before them as Zale ran ahead of her, grabbing her wrist and pulling her with him. Her legs burned. Sudden physical activity made her wheeze. The adrenaline counteracted to move her forward. Rushing through the narrow corridor and out through the door into the main lobby of the castle of illusion.

Aiella willed her eyes to see the concealed door and hallway again in this fortress. Across the way, if she squinted just right, she thought she saw it. Thankfully, her new ally was more confident. Sprinting across the open room, the floor was much slicker below them. Aiella gasped, tumbling backwards. As though predicting it would happen, Zale turned and fell forward to catch her, a loud thud traveling around them. Both scrambling to their feet, they thrust their heads around to ensure no one had seen. Running like the wind, they made it to the hidden passageway quickly just as they heard shouting from outside the looming castle doors. Zale opened the mysterious hidden door, ushering them both inside without a word.

"The world is still worth saving, Zale. It can be beautiful again. Haydn is wrong in thinking he can destroy and control it. He's the problem. We have to help everyone else, too."

Tears streamed down her face unprompted as Zale shut the door behind her swiftly. Glancing around him, she saw a blinking red button. With a nod of approval from Zale, she pressed it, praying for the best. *Please do not be a detonator.* A layer of fog sprayed out, hiding them, and she heard the door lock mechanically. This night was getting weirder.

"I'm glad you feel that way," Zale said. She heard the smile in his voice. "The first part of your name means hope after all." She looked at him quizzically through the thick mist, but he pushed them forward. "Our time is just about up! Come on."

Her feet stayed rooted in place. "Everyone else," she whispered. "We have to help them, too! What if my grandmother is still alive? It might not be too late!" He stepped closer to her so she could see him fully in the haze. His forehead rested on hers, and she shuddered, peaceful energy sparking through her bones. She released the breath she realized she had been clinging on to for the better part of a minute, even through speaking, as he shook his head with a sigh.

"You," he purred. "You are the one we need to save right now. You can't help anyone if you don't save yourself first."

The hot tears were back again, and Aiella wiped them with her sleeve, pulling away from Zale's comforting touch. It agitated her that she was not holding herself together better. Time was running out; she could not afford to grieve right now. The only way she could ever hope to avenge her grandmother and the others Haydn had murdered was to escape out of here alive. The journey that The Elder had been on would not be in vain. She did not have time to think of all the burning queries she had; she had to trust Zale like her grandmother said and get herself out.

She took in the hallway, giving Zale a squeeze on the palm of his hand before they broke out into another run together. Her eyes glided across the pristine windows as she passed. They concealed crystals and strange glowing lights inside them. *And fire.* She stopped in her tracks as she thought about what her grandmother had said. Haydn had started the disease. Created it. She feared that, with her grandmother gone, she might never have the answers to her burning questions. And seeing all of this now... She worried about Zale. She didn't want to leave him. He had so much knowledge of her life she yearned for, and that knowledge would surely land him dead. And that was if Haydn never realized he helped her escape. Her breath became shaky.

She looked in closer to the next window on her right, Zale slowing down to a stop as well. Her stomach clenched instantly. She watched him as he felt all around the surrounding wall for a hidden door hinge, finally feeling a small niche and pulling it aside.

Walking inside, there were half a dozen tanks around the perimeter of the room, all with strange liquids inside of them. Or at least, she thought it looked like liquid. It was thick and glowing, yet seemed insubstantial - like stardust. Etched behind the tanks on the wall were the words "For Aiella's execution."

Becoming more numb by the second, she shuffled around the room, pulling on her clothes and hair, willing an exit to become available. She had to get out of here. Now. She heard a whirring noise and looked above her to the corner of the room. There was a small orange flame, with what looked like golden and black glitter coming off it.

Just then, a booming voice came out of the ceiling, making her jump. "A threatening young woman has escaped, and must be captured at once," she heard Haydn's nasty growl explained to his slaves. She glanced at Zale, who was rummaging through the room even more frantically than she had been. "She has committed crimes punishable by death," the voice continued. "Anyone who sees her is to turn her in to the guards immediately."

Aiella shuddered. "Over here! Time is up!" Zale cried in relief. Ducking down lower to avoid anyone seeing her through the window, she scurried over to where he was in the room. She thought she could see the faint outline of a shape drawing below where he was standing. *A trapdoor,* she thought, *of course!* She bent over and dug her nails into the surface, helping Zale to pry it upward. To her relief, it opened into a dark tunnel. *Now **that** I am used to,* she grinned, feeling like she may have found her advantage. There was hope. As she prepared to jump down, she paused, looking at Zale. Her heart grappled as she realized this was as far as he was joining her.

"He'll kill you. And I am not sure I can do this on my own," Aiella whispered.

"He won't, I'm of too much value... For now." His eyes trailed off into the distance, and Aiella wasn't sure she believed him. He shook his head. "And you can," he replied confidently, his voice barely audible, "You can do it. I am only sad I cannot join you."

"Can't you?" She breathed in the scent of him, closing her eyes, trying to make the rest of the world go away. Why couldn't it go away? She wanted nothing more than...

"Ella?" he asked, tearing her away from her fantasies. She looked at him and nodded, grabbing his hands in hers. He shifted, intertwining their fingers.

"Thank you," she returned, "for everything. I know... We are out of time." As her voice broke, Zale let out a sigh. He pulled her towards him in one sudden movement as he firmly met his lips on hers, his fingers breaking from their grasp on hers and instead entangling themselves in her hair. For the briefest of moments, all of their troubles melted away.

"You have to go. Now," Zale grumbled, releasing her in a swift motion downwards. Holding her with one hand, he grabbed a small, glowing stone out of his pocket with the other, wrapping the chain around Aiella's neck. "Find the truck, get the letter," he instructed. Then, with one last hasty kiss to her cheek, he lowered her quickly into the tunnels.

"Goodbye, Ella." And then he was gone, shutting Aiella in the darkest darkness she had ever known.

She cautiously took a step forward in the pitch-black tunnel, afraid of what booby traps might be set in place, but after a couple of paces, there did not appear to be any. Suddenly aware that she was walking slightly downhill, her exhausted legs felt the force of her weight. She lifted her hands over her head, feeling for a ceiling or walls. The ceiling was right above her head and seemed to get lower, while the walls were a full arm's width away from her. She focused her attention on how far the walls were. Her chest tightened, and even though it was dark, she shut her eyes, desperately heaving in the air. Calming down slowly, she was grateful that the tunnels only seemed to lead in one direction. She shuddered at the thought of twists and turns being a possibility up ahead.

Abruptly, she took a step forward and slipped on a slick, steep surface, stifling a high-pitched yelp. Her entire body lying out on the smooth ground, she tentatively scooted herself forward. A split second later, she was flying through the tunnel.

"Ahhhh!" Aiella screamed, desperately reaching for the surrounding walls, trying to slow down her momentum. Nothing helped; the path was too smooth and steep. She silently prayed that these tunnels were thick, her yelps echoing all around her.

Visions were filling her head, a mix of her past and the present situation she found herself in. Her life was flashing before her eyes as she thought of the many sinister ways that she could die right now. Was she about to fly into the mouth of a monster? Would the tunnel slide suddenly drop into a hole, killing her upon impact? What if it went into another part of the city, one that she couldn't find her bearings in, and got found and sentenced immediately? *Oh gosh, what if there are blades along the sides and bottoms soon? What if this is a setup for those trying to escape?* She cursed at herself in terror, questioning why she trusted random dark tunnels. Her breath became ragged again as she stifled her screams. Nothing seemed to change, the initial shock of her slippery fall subsiding. Even her shallow breathing caused faint echoes off the walls, her fingers covered in a thin, wet film. Visions from ghost stories filled her mind, willing there to be light.

Miraculously, light slowly filled the tunnels as she zipped through. Unsure of the source, Aiella blinked her eyes, gasping. *The crystal.*

The necklace that Zale had placed around her was glowing a brilliant prism of sparks of all colors across her body and onto the walls. Blues and greens danced on the ceiling like an artificial sky over a calming meadow, and golden yellows and reds licked at the ground like magical, harmless flames. In a trance, she imagined this was what it felt like to be a fish under the glistening, mossy river on a sunny day.

Find the truck, get the letter, she thought of Zale saying. She trusted him. Especially given the gift around her neck right now. She shuddered, thinking again of what helping her escape would cost him.

This route was not a trap or setup. If she trusted him, and her grandmother did too, she had to be confident in that. Her mind better at ease, she moved onto the next most likely scenario.

The fortress is on a mountain, overlooking the city and... She stopped mid-thought.

The river. The churning, aggressive, likely *freezing* river.

She realized quickly what the very real outcome of her going downhill for so long was leading to. Why would Zale not prepare her for that!? She shivered and slapped her hands against the tunnel, feeling all around. Panicked, she waved her arms and legs around as fast as she could, hoping for an escape route.

But this was the escape route. Who would expect a need for someone to survive that?

With how small the chute was, and how steep, it was apparent that people were not in mind when building this. No, it must have been for something else. Something else like...

Dread filled her. Likely, this tunnel never crossed anyone's mind as a means to get away. Toxic waste or not, she knew for a fact that this headed to the river, and she was unsure of how much longer she had until she was drowning in the icy currents. She tried to fill her mind with anything distracting, and her lungs with as much foul air as they could fill, attempting to somehow stretch their capacity. She knew it was a long shot.

Before she could put too much planning into it, though, she felt the air grow colder and saw an ever so slightly brighter spot ahead of her.

"This is it," she whispered to herself, bracing for the freezing impact, trying not to think that death was only seconds away. That wasn't an option. She inhaled a deep breath and shut her eyes.

Chapter 14

Aiella shot out into the night like a ball from a cannon. She launched directly into the river, as she had feared. The water chilled her very soul, clawing at her lungs as she opened her eyes, hoping to see which direction to go. Everything was a dark, foggy gray color, illuminated only by the moon and the necklace.

The necklace!

Yards away, she could see the dim glow of the crystal disappearing deep into the river. Thrusting herself deeper, she forced herself further into the depths of the icy water, the swift current threatening to keep her with it forever.

When the bubbles had dissipated from her landing, she could see what she thought was the bottom of the riverbank, the necklace within reach. She snatched it, her arms as heavy as bricks, clinging to it fiercely so it could not fall off again. She smacked her feet against the slanted, mushy service, using every ounce of energy she could muster to push her body upwards. When she thought she was surely going to die, a sudden last burst of energy made her breach the top of the river, and she gasped in as much air as she could. She turned her head, blinking, trying to get a good view of where she was before she became hypothermic. To her solace, she was close to the shore. She whipped her head around, attempting to determine if she could make it across the river to the other side, away from the danger of this place altogether, but she was positive that it was a death sentence. Besides, Zale had given her specific instructions. Squinting across the water, it was apparent there would be no truck on the other bank.

Struggling to the edge of the water, letting the current take her in the direction it felt she needed to go, she felt each bone begin to stiffen more and more. Her body was a rock begging her to go under, and she found herself exhausted enough to consider it. Finally, her shaking hand found damp ground, grasping it until sand was beneath every fingernail. She threw the crystal a few feet away on the shore, coughing profusely. When the coughing subsided, her teeth chattered uncontrollably. She had never felt this cold in her entire life, and she had no way of warming herself. Forcing her rigid, frozen body to join her hands on the bank, she hurled herself to the ground, quick breaths coming in as wheezes as her vision blurred. *This is nice, I could sleep here...* she thought, closing her eyes as the stars twinkled merrily above. She felt her pulse slowing rapidly, wanting nothing more than comfort.

Her arms sprawled outward, too weak to remain on top of her body. Her fingers grazed something hard, and she used her last bit of strength to open her eyes to see what it was.

The crystal was now a different color, not glowing quite as intensely as it had before. Her energy depleted, causing her eyelids to droop involuntarily. The light emanating before her wouldn't allow her to fade, though not entirely. By some sorcery she didn't have the answers to, the longer she stared at the glow through slitted eyes, the more rejuvenated she felt.

Eventually, she had enough strength to fully grab the curious necklace in her palm again. Almost instantaneously, life found its way back into her lungs and blood. Gasping for air like a fish out of water, she convulsed and promptly vomited. Her layers of clothes soaked all the way through, she sat up on the muddy grass forming around her, looking up at the night sky while she continued to shiver and focus on inhaling.

Pulling her legs up to her chest to conserve some of her body heat, she ascertained her submerged clothes were only making it more impossible for her to dry and warm, crystal or not. She scurried to her feet, her hands working shakily to strip off her belongings. *Now is not the time to be modest,* she told herself. Aiella grabbed each item individually and wrung it out the absolute best she could, watching liters of water roll down the bank and back to its flowing mother. She felt like her bones could snap at any given moment, frozen to the very core. She was right, though. Being entirely naked was warmer than having multiple layers of soaked clothing on top of her skin.

Delicately placing the dimly glowing necklace back over her neck, she was immediately thankful for her decision. It was as though millions of tiny fireflies were fluttering into her heart where the stone lay on her. Heat pulsated in waves throughout her, beginning in her chest and blossoming like tiny, hot roots through her veins. Aiella couldn't help but smile at the sensation, throwing her head back in gratitude as a shooting star passed above. Her breathing steadied, she whispered quiet appreciation to Zale, letting the wind carry her message.

Aiella looked up about twenty feet from her and found a small cave-like nook that would at least block her from sight. It should conceal her from any weather misfortunes as well. She considered building herself a fire, her aching body begging her to, but it would be too risky. She could not stay here for long, and so long as she did, she could not draw any type of attention to herself. Trudging up the small hill, she set the dampened clothes down to dry in the wind above the nook and curled herself up underneath. The earth was cold, but she was warming. She inhaled a deep breath of fresh air, content to have another night surrounded by nature. After a time, with the river bubbling peacefully near her, she fell asleep. More vulnerable than she would have ever dreamed could happen, but more alive. Exhausted beyond recognition, she didn't even notice the earth forming around her, softly blanketing her bare body in warm moss.

As morning hit, she sat up, gasping as she rubbed her hands under the earth beneath her. She could have sworn it was only dirt when she fell asleep, but now there was beautiful plush greenery. She shook her head. It was nonsensical to believe it could have grown so rapidly out of nowhere.

When she saw it was still dark, she let herself relax a little, and pulled her clothes off from the hill above in a single swift motion. They were still slightly damp to the touch, but not nearly as wet as they had been earlier. At least she was not shivering as profusely as she had been hours before. In a brief panic, her hand raced to her chest. Aiella released a sigh upon feeling the savior-of-a-crystal around her neck. Noticing it was no longer glowing or warm, she frowned. *How does this work?* She ran in place for a minute and rubbed her hands all over her body as much as she could, trying to create heat from friction. After a few jumping jacks, she quickly put each layer of her clothes on over her, trapping in what little body heat she could. She told herself she should run as much as possible from here on out, at least until it warmed a bit and she knew she was in a safe zone. She looked up at the large city buildings several hundred yards away, and back down at the water, judging which way was east. It would be best to stay as close to the river as possible for now to aid in her direction.

Her breath was rattling and harsh as she sprinted, using up the reserves of her energy a lot faster than she expected. Her lungs burned, if not from the running, then from the memories of water threatening to enter them. She stepped on a rock and yelped, putting a hand over her mouth and hopping on one foot. *Shoot! My other shoe!* She had left her one remaining shoe by the shore when she stripped. Her wound felt crusty and inflamed, and now her other foot was throbbing too. Luckily, she did not feel the warmth of blood dripping from it, so she imagined she only bruised it. Biting her bottom lip to control her frustration and pain, she continued on.

The region of the city by the river was run-down compared to the center of the area—especially when compared to the headquarters of Haydn. She couldn't believe that someone who clearly had so much wealth, paired with an overabundance of resources, could selfishly use it all for himself. Then again, that wasn't even the worst of his crimes.

When she originally found herself in Volcry and contemplated going right, towards the darkness, and away from the city center instead of into the brightly lit buildings, this would have been where she ended up. She remembered stories and books that Frank had informed her of speaking of Depressions and war-torn countries, but she had never seen poverty up close. This place made her home underground look like a luxury. Off in the distance, closer to the more sophisticated structures, she thought she could place the miniature growth of trees that she and her grandmother had hidden in just days before. An overwhelming force echoed for her to go to them, but her logical side knew it would be to no avail. The woods looked torched. Just like her grandmother had been hours before. The striking truth crawled through her very skin, threatening a meltdown, or a plan for vengeance.

Or both.

No, she didn't have time to grieve right now.

Tent-like shacks made of thin sheets and tattered cardboard material lined up, one right after the other. She ran past them on tiptoe, careful not to wake anyone even though she felt confident that, if she did, they would not care in the least that she was there. They probably hated Haydn just as much as she did, given these living arrangements.

Everyone seemed so sickly, and like their minds had never recovered what they lost from the beginning stages of ceremotosis. She could hear ramblings through the tents as she walked on, the idea that everyone was being driven mad or being brainwashed to a degree seeming irrefutable. Though maybe that was what he wanted all along. Perhaps Master Haydn wanted people to blindly follow any orders he set forth so that he could live this delusional life of luxury, blind to the repercussions or morals.

She still could not believe that he had somehow entered her thoughts and even persuaded them in which direction to go. Of all the things that were in this city, and inside that castle, that was the strangest. Suddenly, a grand crimson light shot up into the sky, outwardly reaching into space. She felt a quick shock course through her, just as it had in Spokane. As though there was energy waiting to be released.

Aiella put her hand on her forehead. She felt more tears coming down her face as the fact of The Elder being killed sunk in further. She knew she was short on time, but it felt unfair that she could do nothing to save her; it felt unfair that a guard protected her, having some sort of unearned faith in her. How could she be the person who Haydn had been searching for? Where was he from alongside Zale? None of it made any sense, and it killed her to think about. She wanted nothing more than to discuss all of this with the others at home, but that meant she needed to return home first.

Pushing all the negative thoughts that tried to tell her not to go on while it was still dark, she broke out into a run again. The air was the coldest it had been all night, though refreshing. Wind pricked her exposed skin, forming goosebumps even underneath her clothes. *It must be close to sunrise,* she deduced, both scared and exhilarated to see the sunrise again. Just then, she heard an engine off in the distance. Not quite the whirring that the truck she had ridden here had, but not too far off from it, either. She picked up her pace a bit, trying to find the source of the sound. *Find the truck, get the letter.*

Shutting her eyes for a quick moment to focus, she opened them to an unassuming brick wall, its sole purpose seeming to be a canvas for artists. She halted abruptly to not run straight into it, the placement completely out of the blue. An eerie chill ran down her back as she looked at the painting someone had completed. It was of the earth and the moon, but they were crumbling, with flames engulfing them from all around. Was this how the people of Volcry felt? As though they were constantly burning?

She tilted her head, the sound of an engine purring making her legs walk her around the misplaced wall. Gasping in pleasant surprise, this time it was not an old 21st-century pickup truck before her, but a newer model, with a tall, covered top that latched. It looked like there were chemicals of some sort being placed in the back to be transported. Maybe supplies. Flames licked the bottom side of the vehicle, shooting pulsating shivers down her spine. She looked around the area and saw no one threatening, so she crouched down and approached it slowly, her heart somersaulting in joy when she saw a crate of food in the back. With the sun close to making its full appearance, she quickly boarded while she had the chance. A quiet prayer fell from her lips, hoping this was the path Zale meant for her. Seeing no other trucks around, this was a hunch she could only hope was correct.

Chapter 15

"All right! Everyone ready to go?" A deep and demanding voice boomed. "Master thinks it is time we try to search more than that old Spokane region for relatives of the escaped prisoner to add to our ranks." He snickered. "The Master does not trust his little bots to do a scan on their own again. I would stay put trying to find that escaped girl, but if she landed in that water, she is long gone." He let out a whistle, the others with him giving a chuckle. Aiella did not know whether to breathe a sigh of relief or panic. It seemed like everyone had, in fact, discovered she had escaped through that tunnel into the river. However, she did not feel like anyone down here was taking her search seriously. Definitely benefited her.

She wondered if she should be second-guessing getting on a mode of transportation with people who had been sent to capture her. Maybe this was not the truck that Zale meant. Maybe he had not mentioned a truck at all? Aiella planted her face in her hands, groaning. She couldn't think clearly. Spokane was in the right direction of where she needed to go, though, of that she was certain. It would still be a long journey back to her home from there on foot, one her body couldn't bear to think about right now, but it would be a lot closer than she currently was, and it was ground she had trekked before. She had to do it.

"Damn," she heard one of the passengers said, "I forgot to close the back." Aiella gasped and searched around for somewhere to hide, managing to maneuver herself behind a carton of a pungent liquid right as the man came into sight and slammed the sliding door closed. "All good," she heard him say.

"Good," the main brusque man spoke again. "I don't like when those light beams shoot upwards. Something bad always follows."

The truck started moving forward, Aiella more trapped here than in the pits. Luckily, there were a few holes on each side of the truck walls at the top. She sent her focus to those, watching as the sky gradually lightened outside, and found herself daydreaming. A pastime that, in the past 72 hours, she was unsure she would get to do again.

She was sitting on the edge of a lake, watching a woman gather pebbles for her to throw inside. The woman was beautiful, with a face that did not smile but still somehow emanated love and happiness. "Ai," she said soothingly, bringing the pebbles to her. "Look, you can throw them like this." She tossed the rocks into the water, Aiella in awe at the ripples that formed. It was a gorgeous day, the sun was shining much like it was right now, and it felt like it was early springtime too. She stood and grabbed a rock in her tiny hands, and threw it with all of her might, so proud when it made it to the water's surface. "Good job, Ella baby," the woman told her. She heard her added in under her breath, "we will protect you first." Across the way, little Aiella pointed in awe at the red clouds swirling over a large volcano.

Aiella blinked, the sky through the holes a brilliant blue with no red clouds in sight. At least not through her limited line of vision. She was viewing the world through a hole, never fully able to enjoy it. Not like she enjoyed it back then...

She felt a pang in her head and chest, feeling suffocated at the revelation that what she had just been thinking about may actually be a memory.

"That woman was my mom," she whispered out loud to herself, her relaxed thoughts becoming chaos once again. *What did she mean, protect me first?* She thought about this new potential memory of life before she lost her mother, paired with all the new information she recently came upon. Haydn. The tree. The crystal. The Elder being her grandmother. Zale. She wanted to cry in frustration, clearly heading home with more questions than she left with. She wished she hadn't left the comfort of her tribe's tunnels. How was she going to tell them all that The Elder was dead? Maybe ignorance could be bliss.

She absentmindedly twirled the stone necklace in her fingers, numbness setting in, pondering what science must be making it work. Frank was going to have a field day when she returned with it! *Frank.* What was he going to say about her leaving? Had he known all along that The Elder was her blood relative?

Was Zale was being punished for letting her go? She let her mind fixate on the thought of him sweeping her up in his arms, and running off into the sunset with her. They could both be safe. She had always been a romantic, wanting to believe in fairytale love stories, but sadly knowing they were not realistic. Not in this day and age. She shook her head, forcing herself to recall the informative parts of her journey. Boy, the stories she would tell Alexis and Luke...

She felt the truck bouncing around on roads that were hardly used anymore, ones with no more stories of adventure. *There are more people than just us,* she reminded herself. That wasn't all bad. They may be broken, burned, and all under the ruling of an evil tyrant, but *there were other people.* They needed saving, clearly brainwashed into their current states, idolizing Haydn, who would kill them with joy if needed. Letting that sink in fully, she let out a gasp, sinking further against the back of the truck.

She needed to let her mind and body fully rest while it could and talk to Frank about everything once she got back home; it was too overwhelming to sift through all on her own. Her stomach grumbled a warning; Aiella's attention lustfully focused on the thirst and hunger she was feeling. She slowly forced herself to be propped up, looking around at the crates in the back with her. They couldn't have been on the road for more than an hour so far. The drive down here had seemed to take forever, although she supposed this was a different vehicle. Regardless, she felt she was safe to quietly shuffle through the boxes to find something edible to eat or drink, their destination likely being far off still.

After a few minutes of browsing as silently as she knew how, she was pleased to find a canteen of water and a box of bread. She chugged the drink and savored a handful of the food in a few slow bites. She continued to rummage around her, hoping to find something that could assist with having no supplies while also trying to find more food she could bring home. At that point, it would be for her family.

She returned her gaze up to the top of the truck walls again, suddenly hearing something akin to large balls hitting all around. She instinctively held her arms over her head, scared whatever it is might break through.

"That son of a bitch!" One man from the front shouted, slamming the steering wheel. "He thinks he can play God or something, and he is going to get us all killed."

Aiella was stunned, wondering what on earth he was talking about. Then, as she looked up outside, she saw the ever-slightest tinge of orange in the massive ice block hitting the truck. *Hail.* She had never heard of any quite like this. Ice was freezing. It should not have trails of fire coming off of it. There was a lot she had read about that she had not witnessed herself until this week. She did not know if she should laugh or cry about her luck.

"Is this fiery hail from that bright beam we saw at his fortress before we left?" Aiella heard one of the truck passengers ask.

The boss's voice got harder to hear over the booming weather, so Aiella pressed her ear as close as she could to the truck bed wall. "Yes, I think it is. Ever since we all got healed, haven't either of you wondered what was on the agenda for our Master Haydn? Given the slums he has us all serving him from–no matter our rank–you know he did not do it out of goodwill. He has something hidden."

Aiella could feel the mood in the entire truck change, the hardness of these monsters seeming to change. She no longer viewed them as threatening as before, realizing all of these people were human, and humans merely did what they had to in order to survive. Right? Her feelings towards them softened as he continued to talk to his peers. "There are rumors that he is from the eastern sector."

"What does that have to do with anything?"

"Everything," he responded plainly. "That is where it is believed the whole ceremotosis outbreak began." Aiella shuddered, the knowledge that Haydn created it making her uneasy. If those rumors held to be true, maybe others would as well. She pushed the side of her face even harder into the metal, willing it to hear more. "Have either of you ever been to his lab?" She heard him ask.

"He has a lab?" One asked back incredulously.

"Hidden in his castle of a home," he replied. Aiella wondered if he meant the hallway she had been down to escape. It seemed akin to a lab, especially with the strange liquid meant just for her execution... "The light that beams upward every so often—I have a gut feeling it comes from there. Whether it is on purpose, or if anyone can fully comprehend it, is beyond me." A larger piece of hail hit, sending them swerving. "Dammit," she heard him mutter. Straightening the truck out, it seemed their conversation was over, so Aiella went back to her hiding place and slumped against a crate, cradling more bread on her lap, mindlessly eating. She just wanted to be home already. Fiddling around with more bread, she was about to toss the wrappings of the food out of the crate when a folded piece of paper fell into her lap.

Dearest Aiella,

If you have found this, that means you have made it safely to your transportation towards your loved ones. It also means you have found food to eat, which is good. I know you have quite the appetite.

What looked like a winking face was next to it, alongside a drawing of a girl attacking a boy for water. She couldn't help but laugh, her chest aching to think about what could be happening to Zale right now.

All jokes aside, I must apologize to you. I am sorry that I could not explain more to you while you were here. There are few places that are safe, and within the walls of the fortress is not one of them. I wish I could have explained everything, so you understood.

There is not much time, so I will get to the point. I am a special operative on the Elemental Council. I know you do not know what that is right now, and again I am sorry I cannot explain more. Just know this: You saved me. As a spy for the good guys of Satera, I have been at the serving hand of Haydn for many years, waiting for a sign. I was so close to finally becoming fully corrupted. But you saved me. You gave me hope. You ARE hope. Your grandmother may think she failed at her mission, but if you found this, she did not. She will always be in my heart, too.

Please stay safe. Keep the necklace close. Soon, you will have the answers you are searching for.

Signed,

Zale

P.S. I really hope I had the guts to kiss you. Til next time.

Aiella read the letter over again. And again. Clinging it to her chest, she looked out through the small opening in the wall again, clear skies once again forming. She would have to ask Frank and some of the others where Satera was, what country or sector it was a part of. It had to be Eastern. A deep whirring ignited inside of her, knowing that Satera was where she was from as well.

A few hours later, Aiella finally felt the vehicle come to a full stop. Her newest curiosity was trying to piece together how the truck was able to even run, though she kept reminding herself that other alternative forms of fuel had taken over by the end of the 21st century. Surely, these ran off something more sophisticated, regardless of what year they may have been manufactured. Her brain kept buzzing and telling her it had to do with the odd power source that Haydn harnessed.

When she was about eight, Frank started giving her science lessons using different textbooks from his college career. Her favorite was and remained to be, chemistry. He tried to teach Alexis and Luke as well, but they never were nearly as interested. Aiella loved it all. By age ten, she had memorized the periodic table in its entirety, having nothing better to do than learn. By the time she was a teenager, she knew more than most university graduates had, as Frank tirelessly told her and everyone else at home. She always found the chapters on spectroscopy to be fascinating, too, and pictured herself as a scientist studying beams of light and color interacting with each other.

She knew all the properties of every known element on the planet, and everything possible about air and the earth. All thanks to Frank's textbooks. However, the more she thought about it, the more she had no idea where to place the strange power source she had seen inside the lab. She had no idea what to make of the flash of light that the drivers spoke of, or the tinted hail that later fell from the sky. The necklace around her was its own mystery. Frank would have a field day when he heard about all of this, as would her young friends. Eli crossed her mind. Her heart shriveled at the thought of him finding out that she had kissed Zale, no matter how briefly. She was always so guarded, never letting herself open up. Especially not of her feelings for him buried deep inside of her, and she knew it would break him to think she tried to with someone else. She shook her head, brushing off any and all emotion for the time being. There was never a reason Eli would even need to find out. They were just friends. Besides that, it was not like it was likely Ella would ever see Zale again.

Chapter 16

Deep in thought, she almost forgot that the truck had come to a stop until she heard footsteps and the door to the truck back being lifted. She crouched down as low as she could but was no longer confident that she would stay concealed. There was an abundance of boxes and crates to unload in front of her, and the men did just that while making small talk. Since the hail had stopped abruptly when they were driving, it made her feel like they had been inside their own weather system. She believed what the boss of this task had told his subordinates about the beam of light likely caused by Haydn more and more. Was it his way of trying to find her?

"What the hell!" One of them yelled, freezing Aiella in her awkward position, wishing she could be invisible. *Please don't be me,* she pleaded silently, fear creeping into her mind that she had been spotted. She was too afraid to glance up and see if they were looking at her.

"Boss, you better come over here."

"What now?" She heard him demand grumpily. He walked over. Silence. She gulped; surely, she was caught. Someone else was inside the truck with her, their steps making the ground beneath her vibrate. She nervously glanced up from her knees, right into the eyes of the head of this expedition.

"Who are you?" He asked. Aiella jumped up, ready to attack or run if needed.

"Don't kill me!" she shouted. "I am not a threat. I just want to go home, and... And he was after me."

"Look, I'm not—"

She jumped up; his hand extended too close to her.

"Don't touch me!" She shouted, trying to shove herself away from him. It was a lost cause.

At her sudden movement, the three men in front of her put their hands to their waists. Weapons? Without hesitating to find out, Aiella grabbed the now-empty crate she found her bread inside and hurled it towards the man that stood in the large truck with her. He stumbled backwards, his head hitting the metal that lined the bed, cursing loudly as his hand made its way to his ear. It was bleeding.

Almost had him out of the truck completely. But almost didn't matter. He was still in front of her, and he was surely armed. She was not. Her mind racing a million miles a minute, she scanned her eyes as rapidly as her body would allow for some form of defense. Why hadn't she thought this part of the journey through? Why hadn't Zale? Her heart sank momentarily, thinking that he may have betrayed her being too much to bear.

No.

He wouldn't have done that. Why would he go through the effort of getting her out of Haydn's grasps only to have her murdered a day's trip away? Besides, her grandmother trusted him, too.

"So you want to fight, eh?" the man in the truck said as he stood up slowly. His shoulders hunched over as he balled his fists. He wasn't as large in build as, say, Eli, but he was still terrifying to think of fighting. Frantically, she searched one last time around her for a weapon to defend herself. *Aha!*

Lunging with the force of her entire body, Aiella clambered over one of the wooden crates, just barely reaching a long pole with a torch on top of it. A sharp metal torch. Not having time to learn how the fire worked right now, she swung the object over her head. In a maneuver that usually was done with a branch to frighten away predatory animals, the cresset slammed across the man's chest, a sickening crunch filling the air as he howled in pain. He keeled over immediately, screaming at his partners to take revenge.

"What are you waiting for!" he yelled, his voice breaking at the end. "Get her!"

She needed to escape. And she needed to escape now. The walls of the back of the vehicle felt like they were shrinking in on her as she scooted backwards towards her original hiding place. With her eyes still on the enemy, she crouched down, snagging the few provisions she had found while scurrying around. She let out a sigh; how would she carry this all?

Then she saw it: a tarp. A large, albeit dirty, piece of material was hanging haphazardly on one of the walls, blending in so that it was hardly noticeable. In a split second, she flung the torch around her head to the wall, scraping the tapestry gracefully off the surface in one swift motion. Looking up, she saw that while the main enemy was still down, the other two men were now climbing aboard the truck. Figuring she only had ten seconds until an attack, she worked methodologically tossing the bread and every other provision and trinket she could quickly manage into the bag and twisting it into a knot over her shoulder.

The men were right before her, waving around strange blades that appeared to be glowing.

"We can't let you get away, Miss," one of them said. *Miss?*

"How polite you are," Aiella replied with a snort. She wasted no time speedily knocking him to the ground, the torch meeting him between the legs. With the side of the truck he had been on now open as he wailed onto the ground, Aiella leaped over the boxes between her and the man. She scurried against the wall, jumping over the crying man with pity and keeping her focus on the one still standing. She quickened her pace and bounded off the end of the cargo bed.

Before she felt her feet hit the ground, though, a hand grasped her ankle. Instead of her foot landing, her head and arm took the brunt of the fall, blood immediately gushing from near her eyebrow. Her shoulder felt like it was on fire. With a grunt, she used the back end of the torch to stab his hand, releasing her from his clutches with a growl.

The two assistants now both stood in the back of the truck again.

"Why won't you fight her?!" the head man screamed. "Kill her!"

"But we can't kill her, Lad," one of them objected. Aiella stood up slowly, taking steps back as she did.

"Why not?" The man - presumably Lad - said through gritted teeth.

"M-Master Haydn. He would not approve. We must just capture her." Lad sneered at him, leaning over onto him to steady himself and stand. Then he violently pushed him. The man tumbled to the ground, crashing into the crates. His head hit the corner of the one she had pushed aside, his eyes shutting instantaneously. Aiella shuddered. If he was willing to do that to someone he worked with, she didn't want to see what he could do to her.

Turning completely around, she ran. The breeze whipped around her face, giving her a newfound energy, before she suddenly tumbled to the ground.

"Argh!" Aiella gasped as she withered in pain on the hard ground. The torch and the makeshift knapsack of goodies were a few yards ahead of her, scattered on the ground. Choking in affliction, she rolled onto her back, her breaths becoming more labored. Her heartbeat quickened as she felt warm blood pooling all around her. Her hand went first to her head, which was still bleeding. It wasn't enough to cause... this. Running her fingers down the length of her body, she twinged in discomfort. Shakily, she forced herself to look at her side.

A large handle of a blade was sticking out of her flesh.

Aiella's breathing turned into wheezing as she screamed out in pain.

"Sucks when you're the one losing, doesn't it?" Lad asked with a twisted grin on his face. He was too much like Haydn. Aiella's insides squirmed, her vision becoming blurred.

"I'm not... losing," she puffed. No matter how much it felt like it.

"Sure seems like it," he replied plainly. The vehicle was running now and ready to leave. To bring her back to Haydn. In this state. He was right; she was losing. She could never hope to get out of his grasp alive like this.

"Why are you doing this?" She managed to gasp out.

"Doing what?" He responded.

"This. Capturing me... working for him. He's a monster."

"You know..." Lad told her, closing the distance between them as he squat down. "You're really not in a position to be asking questions right now." He looked at the knife lodged in her side. With a look that could almost pass as apologetic, he took it out. Instantly the pain eased, but something worse replaced it. She was going to faint. It was too much blood. She'd die right here.

"I think now may be the best time," she retorted weakly, her eyes fluttering shut against her will, though her mind was gaining back its edge. This was her territory. She could not perish like this. "I have nothing... to lose..." Her body wanted desperately to sleep, but she knew if she caved, she might never wake up. For the first time, she got a better look at her newest captor. He seemed as though he got the antidote promptly following his diagnosis and did not have to suffer nearly as badly as some others in Volcry. In many ways, he looked completely fine, just with a few nasty scars along his upper body from what she could tell. Surprisingly, there were no marks on his face. Given how Haydn had responded to her face being free from fault, she could not imagine that there were many others like him. From what she had seen and heard, most occupants of the city Haydn reigned control over were on the edge of death before he saved them from their ultimate demise. Did he know him personally?

"Well, I have everything to lose, and everything to gain," he returned. Her vision was fading in and out now. She didn't have much time, her entire being setting into a state of panic.

"Humor me," she choked out. She couldn't differentiate reality from fantasy right now, but she thought she heard a chuckle.

"All right," he told her. "I suppose it won't matter much when you're dead." Aiella did her best to focus on every syllable he spoke. *Just hang in there a few more minutes,* she pleaded with herself. Focus on the words. Stall. She could feel the crystal, concealed beneath her shirt, starting to soak into her, a warm energy surging into her heart. Lad appeared to glance nervously back at the truck before he spoke again. Did he really think the others would turn him in against Haydn?

"I've heard you didn't think others, like all of us in Volcry, were alive. A bold assumption. There are many people still out there.

Most working towards a common goal. About ten years ago, this Pacific Northwest sector started to exhibit symptoms of the disease as well. Many of us called it the plague of the 22nd century, and there were hundreds, if not thousands, of people who committed suicide as soon as word of it reaching this side of the country got out. The news channels had shown how gruesome it was in the beginning. That was before travel and forms of communication became less and less available. The East had always been the most populated, and we didn't feel as crowded over here. We thought with quarantines in place, we would all be safe. But ceremotosis, as you know, is something else.

"Within only a couple of months of word getting out, everyone's lives began being destroyed. Some fled, which only caused more devastation for more people, and some even started to climb to the tops of mountains with sleighs full of supplies to make shelter underground and away from the rest of the common population." She was silent, slowly drifting away. He continued, holding himself tall as a hidden softness took him over.

"A lot of us tried to do that. But what many did not think about was: if everyone was doing that, nowhere was all that safe, especially the closer you were to the cities. It became a matter of luck. Many perished, if not from the disease, then by nature. Not accustomed to living in the wild and having no survival skills. That part was critical. I am sure it became a full-spread pandemic after people fled. We all should have been better prepared, but we were naïve.

"Eventually, the few groups of people left had to come out of hiding, running out of resources, and at some point those of us in what once was good ole Oregon started to stumble into the presence of Master Haydn. He was not diseased. He spoke of hope. He claimed to have a way to make all of us invincible. It sounded great, like we all had a chance. He took biological samples of all of us wanting to enter his city. He claimed it was like no other.

"We had high hopes, but it did not matter much. Once inside, and he had it blocked off very well from the borders at first, we saw nothing but shambles and little to work with in terms of careers or making a living. Or even building a life again. Many fell very ill, very fast, which is why the first conspiracy theories of him diseasing us were born. Master Haydn, as promised, had an antidote, though. He gave it to everyone as they were clinging to the last straws of life. No one ever fully healed. The progress of the disease was stopped in its tracks, something we all are grateful for, but still we were left with all the irreparable damage. I got out of it almost unscathed. Unlike others.

"Not that it matters, but if you go against him... You disappear. Zale told me that old Aggie passed a few days ago, and that one hit all of us deep." Lad's voice got more shallow. "She was my great aunt, though many don't know that. Executed a few days back at sundown. You don't find many families that have multiple surviving relatives..."

"I'm sorry to hear that," Aiella tried to say, but mostly sputters came out. That was the old lady she had seen at the city center. Her heart felt like knives were diving into it. You wouldn't think that after battling that horrendous disease, something worse could be out there. *I wish it would all go back to how it was,* she thought. Ignorance certainly sounded like bliss right about now. She slowly opened her eyes, using every last shred of energy she could muster, finding Lad's face observing her.

"I can't die here. You know that," she whispered slowly. "He... He would kill you." Lad cocked his head to one side, a spark flashing across his eyes. He looked back at the vehicle again.

"Stay here," he suddenly told her, rushing back to the truck. With her eyes shut alongside her willpower, the world turning dark and quiet, a strange sensation lit up in her side. She was paralyzed to the spot, but she was healing! He had used the serum Zale had in her cell.

Her plan had worked. She reached his humanity.

"Now I'll live. And you." Lad said. "Until you get to Haydn." He grabbed hold of both of her legs and began to drag her to the truck. Her back screamed in turmoil, but then the ground became much softer. She scanned the dirt around her to see it wasn't dirt at all, but grass and moss blossoming like a protective layer below her.

"What the...?" Lad questioned the scenery in front of him, but couldn't finish his sentence before a small crevice appeared behind him, causing him to trip and tumble backwards onto the truck. His head hit the latch on the back, knocking him unconscious. Aiella wasted no time. She used the energy coursing into her from the strange crystal, bolted up, and ran, only pausing briefly to grab her new torch and fallen items.

She was free again.

Chapter 17

Who am I?

Aiella broke out into a run, letting the buildings and monuments blur far behind her, tears burning her eyes.

She made it a lot further than she thought she would by the time she stopped running; she was already within the edge of the forest, with the ever-familiar creek in sight. A tremendous weight lifted off her as it forced her to acknowledge that she was nearly home. She imagined that if she ran, or at least jogged, she could make it back to her loved ones just after dark. Judging by the position of the sun, she should have a couple of hours of daylight left, perhaps less from the shaded canopy of trees. Inhaling, she started at a slow walking pace, gaining her stamina again, and then bolted again through the trees, winding along the small river.

Not much later, Aiella paused her trek briefly to look at everything she had stolen for her one-woman trek back through the forest. Back *home*. She saw the three loaves of bread that she had unwrapped earlier, and her heart filled with happiness. If she could return by tomorrow, she could share these baked goods with the people who meant the most to her for breakfast. It felt like it had been so much longer than just a week since she had talked to them last. Tomorrow seemed too far off, but she knew with the amount of energy she had paired with her healing injury, that pushing herself might not be the smartest option. Still...

She sat down on a rock, only noticing now that her knee was bouncing, with her arms shaking.

"I miss my family," she admitted aloud, rubbing her hands together and looking at what else she had gathered. No matter his motives, she would forever be grateful to Lad for deciding to heal her. He helped her live to return to her family, whether he liked it, and it spoke volumes. Haydn was a master of manipulation.

In her few-second dash, she didn't know what she had grabbed, but she was pleased with herself now that she saw and could think clearly. A knife, like the one that had impaled her, was wrapped inside a fresh shirt. There were a few other trinkets, such as a strange, round light source, that Aiella was sure would impress the tribe.

The clothes she had taken out for her smelled like dirt but looked pristinely clean. More importantly, they were soft and very warm. In the sunshine, she would overheat, but the day was already on its last leg, and Aiella was strongly considering walking straight through the night as she pulled the delicate material over her head. She would have a couple of hours of daylight still, at least. Maybe more.

Wanting to use it for its actual purpose, she scanned the floor for a long stick to use in place of the torch for her makeshift knapsack. Aiella smiled as she found just the right branch up ahead. Snagging it and circling back to her belongings, she focused her thoughts on Zale while she re-tied her sack. The serum! She had ended up with some of it, as well. Hopefully, one day, she saw the guard again. She briefly brushed a hand to her chest, double-checking that both the letter and necklace from him were still underneath her shirt. Her heart fluttered, her fingers finding their way to her lips as she shut her eyes in blissful memory. Even though they had just met, it felt like they had connected on a level she couldn't explain. Nevertheless, friendly human contact was about to be her norm again, and for that, she was grateful. She took a deep breath, refreshing her mind for the rest of the tiresome hike she was about to embark on.

She grabbed her new sack and threw it over her shoulder again. The torch could now be used as a walking stick. She still didn't know how to light it, but figured she should start walking, anyway. A sigh escaped her. Hopefully, there were no cougars out today. Dusk was always a risky time for wildlife encounters.

She couldn't help but wonder if Lad had a spouse or children before the outbreak. He seemed old enough. She wondered if that would make her feel better, or worse. Everything seemed so silent out here compared to the chants of the execution and the purring engine of the truck. As terrible a city as Volcry had been to her, there was a strange gaping hole forming within her. Did she miss it? It was hard not to be enamored by the newfound world. No...

Conflicted was the better word. She inhaled, and without looking back, let herself imagine she was flying.

It was just her and nature again.

As the sun was sinking away for the day, Aiella was impressed with her adrenaline for keeping her as alert and active as it had. Even with the sack over her shoulder, she felt light on her feet. Stamina should have been the last thing she had, but she was free. Finally, free after days of feeling like she would rot away, hidden from the rest of the world with no answers.

She felt buzzing.

Looking down, the crystal was burning bright again, a smile creeping onto Aiella's face. *It's giving me extra energy.* She relished all that she had learned from Zale and her grandmother Athena. Even Lad and his gang had given her some insight, even if coerced. Bottom line, she was happy she had gained *something* from this trek. Even if The Elder was not returning home with her.

She wrapped her fingers around the letter tucked close to her, inhaling deeply, trying to accept how everything had turned out. At least she had something that she could share with the others when she got home. Home... She was going to return home! Aiella paused, looking up towards the colorful sky and whispering to the heavens. "Thank you, Grandmother. You did not die without purpose."

Briefly, she considered turning back, unwilling to accept that the entire city was being held prisoner. It amazed her that Zale had helped her at all in that dark fortress of secrets. How had her grandmother known about him? She felt a prickling on her neck, thinking about the fact that her grandmother's arrival had been expected in Volcry. Inevitable. What was her mission, and how had Aiella and Zale apparently accomplished it, anyway? She heard a branch snap somewhere behind her and to the left, in the denser region of the forest, and promptly lost all thoughts about what had happened, allowing herself to enter survival mode again. More adrenaline. More energy from her crystalline ally. She kept pushing on.

As night fell, she judged she did not have much longer to go. An ebb of happiness and hope began to form within her as soon as she finally lit the torch. After many frustrating minutes of no cooperation, she finally settled on building a fire first and trying to light the torch from there. To her astonishment, it worked! The flame, however, was a strange anomaly. It grew and then shrank, seeming to float above the metal instead of being lit from within it. The color was off, too. It wasn't simply red and orange, or even slightly blue. It was every color. The flaming ball in the center was red and orange, but it was as though it was a contained comet - small tails of multiple colors dancing up from it. *Frank and the others will be so intrigued.* After successfully lighting it, she held it out to her side, walking cautiously at first, watching how the ember waned as it became bigger and then curled back up over and over. She was both enthralled and terrified by it. Something about it reminded her too much of Haydn.

She shuddered, stopping to focus on what had happened in her questioning for the first time since it had happened. Of course, the torch was one of Haydn's inventions. She considered throwing it away right then and there. The traumatic memory of her questioning and imprisonment was too painful, and she wanted to block it out, but she couldn't. *Why did I feel the pain of the tree burning?* She winced, the sparks before her causing her to endure it all over again. She clenched her eyes shut, focusing. It hadn't been the first time, just never to that degree. Haydn had known she would react that way, and deep down, she did too. While scavenging, she had sliced into plants wrong plenty of times, the pain always inflicting her alongside them. Living nature being damaged brought her physical pain. It was a fact. But *why?*

She compelled her pensive thoughts to melt away and jogged. Albeit awkwardly, with the fire contraption in one hand, and her bundle of belongings over her body in the other. She was afraid that if she broke out into a run again, the knapsack would somehow burst into flames. She was sure the logic was flawed, but she feared it engulfing her. Would she ever recover from this trip? Did anyone ever recover from the damage Haydn had done?

She found familiar markings on trees shortly after, tempted to yelp in relieved joy. She was getting close! This was within her range of a normal, short hunting and gathering trip—usually the type she would make in the winter when the elements were more threatening. Aiella slowed her pace, allowing herself to take everything in. Her body, now that it knew it was almost home, was begging to be given a break, maybe forever. It took everything in her to continue on that last mile or so, making overwhelmingly slower progress than she had before. What would she say to the others as soon as she arrived? She pleaded silently again and again that everyone would be there, and not gone looking for her. That worried her more than anything.

She lifted her shirt up briefly, the skin on her side a tender scar. She was marked now, like all the ceremotosis victims of Volcry after her incidents with Lad and Haydn. Yet another silent prayer filled her head, pleading that Frank was following his protocol of not leaving to look for others if they had been missing. She was sure the internal conflict he was facing from not knowing if she was still alive was more of a struggle than her physical trials. She thought she might throw up from guilt, but then a familiar line of bushes and trees came into view in the light of the fiery stick.

Aiella arrived at the entrance of the tunnels and knocked her heels into the door on the ground, hoping someone would still be awake to open it for her since her hands were full and exhaustion was overtaking her more every second. Or maybe she just hoped that people were on standby, desperate to see a friendly face. After a minute of no response, she turned to set her new belongings on the ground beside her, careful to still hold the torch upright. To her delight, she heard a creaking behind her. She spun around, Frank poking his head out of the ground.

"Frank!" she yelled, dashing to the door in a few giant leaps.

"Ella?" he asked, choking back tears. "I can't believe you're home! You're alive!"

"I'm sorry I worried you," she said solemnly, "I--"

"Oh, none of that!" he cut her off. "Come on down! Home! You must be tired." Nodding vigorously, she grabbed her sack and threw it down the hatch door, clambering inside with her torch once Frank was safely on the ground. She pulled the door down overhead and let it drop shut as she descended. Never in her life had she been this thankful or relieved. She had made it *home.*

As soon as they entered the doorway into the living area, Alexis threw herself into her arms. Surprisingly, no smoke emanated from the torch as she smothered it.

"I am so happy you're home!" Alexis cried.

"We thought we might never see you again," Luke added in behind her, giving a smile. She saw Eli leaning against the opposite wall, watching the scene unfold in front of him. Aiella gave him a warm smile, but he got up and left the room. Frank, Alexis, and Luke looked back around at her, clearly having watched Eli leave. They were the only four in the room.

"The others all got in bed," Frank explained. "Just the four of us were up, hopeful you might return home. Eli was really close to leaving to come find you, you know." Her stomach tightened. No wonder he left the room. She should have told him her plans before she left. Her wrongdoing overtook her, her mind going in zig zags. Eli was her best friend, and life was too short. Aiella sighed, her heart rate feeling oddly labored.

"I'll be right back. Bathroom. Been a long day," she said unconvincingly, walking briskly out of the room. Eli was about to cross through the kitchen doorway into the sleeping chambers. "Wait," she whispered desperately. The curtain separating the rooms dropped out of his hands, and he turned to her with heavy eyes, biting his bottom lip in a way that made her tingle.

"You should've told me what you were planning. I was so worried--"

Aiella forgot about everything else and ran across the small room to him, pressing her body against his in one smooth motion, breathing him in.

"I missed you," she whispered.

He hesitated in surprise for a moment, but then fiercely returned the intimate hug, his arms embracing her as tightly as they could, his fingers twitching with longing.

Their moment together ended too quickly, and she walked back out into the living room, a massive headache beginning to force its way to her. The air in here was welcoming and warm, but felt heavier and more suffocating than usual after being in fresh air for a while.

She wanted badly to curl up in warmth and sleep for the next decade. She wanted to take a magic pill or drink some magic potion that could make her forget everything she had done and seen in the past week. Maybe the necklace could do that.

Gazing in front of her at Frank and the others, she nodded to the couch in the room. They had started going through her sack, likely recognizing it was foreign, and their faces were completely blank in confusion. Frank looked like he wanted to say a lot but was unsure where to start. Luke looked lost entirely, and Alexis appeared flat out terrified. Aiella herself wasn't even sure where to begin, but there was no point in holding anything off. Not when they saw what she brought back. Not when they were worried, she was dead. Not when she was lucky to even be alive. She owed the people in front of her an explanation as soon as possible, and a full, truthful one at that. The time had to be now, but she felt like she owed the people of that corrupted city some sort of help, too. She wanted to cry. To quit. To dig herself into a deeper hole. Being back home was making her too introspective. She shook her head. There was no time for moping.

"I see you found my new knapsack," she started, a laugh hidden somewhere in there, wanting to come out to help lighten the mood.

"Where have you been, Ella?" Frank whispered. He struggled the next words out. "*Who* were you with? Did you find her?" His eyes were wide, and she felt the three of them mutually shudder, never in their wildest dreams expecting the stories that were about to pour out of her mouth. This was her last chance to save them from the knowledge of the true horror out there, but that would mean taking from them the bits and pieces of beauty as well, for they went hand in hand. No, she would tell them everything.

"Well," Aiella said, her mouth feeling drier than it had in the pits, "we are not the only humans left around here." Alexis gasped, putting her hand to her face, while Luke and Frank both stared at her, their jaws dropping slightly. "And... The Elder is dead." She had their full attention, against her deepest wishes. Alexis let out a stifled sob, covering her face as Luke protectively embraced her.

"No," Frank said, his face paling. "That can't be. Ella, she was your--"

"Grandmother," she finished for him. "I figured you probably knew."

"I never meant to keep it from you," he whispered, his eyes wide and full of water. "She said she was going to tell you when the time was right, and then when she disappeared, I didn't want to cause you more pain. Especially after learning about your immunity. I just wanted to give you time. I didn't want you to think you lost someone even closer to you than you realized, and then you went looking for her..." He looked at her, his gaze pleading with hers as though he needed forgiving. She ran to him, letting him wrap her in his fatherly arms and breaking down.

"I tried to bring her home," she finally cried. "I found her. I found her, and she was well. I tried to bring her home." Her body shook uncontrollably with sobs. She gasped for air between quiet wails, looking at Alexis and seeing she was having the same fit as her, both the boys' eyes glossy as well. Sniffles filled the air.

"May she rest in peace," Frank said, his voice cracking. They all nodded, letting themselves meltdown and mourn.

Chapter 18

When she felt she had no more energy or tears left in her, Aiella let go of Frank, standing tall.

"My grandmother did not die in vain," she whispered, shaking her head. Memories flooded her of their time in the city, in their mini orchard of trees, the way she so willingly sacrificed her life to allow time for planning for Aiella to get away, the look in The Elder's eyes before she was dragged off to her execution. She turned to face the others, heaving in a broken breath and finding a seat on the sofa. She placed her head in her hands, rocking back and forth.

"I never thought that I would stumble upon what I did. I was inside one of the broken-down stores in the downtown region of Spokane and stepped on a broken piece of the window. The metal and glass got lodged in my foot." She gestured down to her heel, still cut up since the soft scar had more damage done to it. Alexis winced through her sniffles. "That's when I heard something outside. I looked up, and there was a vehicle. An old twenty-first century truck it looked like from pictures I've seen. I climbed into the back, and then it *started moving*. I was so scared, I made myself flat against the ground of the back of the truck and held on. Once I came to my senses, it occurred to me I should jump off, but we were going too fast. As it turned out: tiny robots were driving it. I had landed myself in a truck being driven by the smallest of androids. I don't even know what the extent is of what they can do…" She trailed off. What were those androids for?

"I ended up in an alleyway, far, far away. We were driving for at least a few hours. I got out of the truck to find food and water for my long journey back home, and that's when I realized I was in a city. I later learned the name is Volcry." Frank gasped, and she gave him a quizzical look.

"It can't be true," he breathed.

"What?" Aiella asked, leaning forward.

"She had talked about that city," he admitted, looking her directly in the eye. With his forehead wrinkled, his lips quivering.

"It's okay," she told him, knowing he meant to apologize for keeping so much from her.

"You could have died because of the secrets I kept from you, Ella," he murmured.

"But I didn't," she stated. After all she had seen, there was no room for grudges. Life was too fragile. "The leader is called Master Haydn. He lured the citizens in with a type of antidote available that stops the progression of the disease in its tracks. He diseased them all, then gave them the cure right before they died. It merely stops the damage in its tracks, never reversing it. As such, most of them suffer from wounds of varying degrees.

"They serve him and his every whim, those against him being sentenced to death immediately, and those who do serve him being treated to poor living conditions. They are slaves. It's as if this wealthy man had a ton of resources and just wanted to build an empire in which he was the complete center of attention and treated like a king. He's disgusting." She spat out the last words like a bad piece of meat, her family looking at her, their curiosity piqued. "There are banners hung all around stating he is a hero, but he burned an elderly woman alive in front of the entire city the night I arrived. And that's what he does three times a day on average. A few days later... It was The Elder's turn." They all locked eyes, letting out a unified moan of sorrow.

"She found me while I was watching the execution," Aiella continued shakily. "She ushered me to a safe place she had on the edge of the city. A small enclosure of trees. She read a note that was pinned to the bark, and it must have been a warning."

"What did it say?" Luke queried.

"I'm not sure," she responded sadly. "But she took off in the direction of guards coming our way so that I could escape. Master Haydn knew where to find me, though. I was captured within minutes, and so was she. Thankfully, the guard ushering me between questioning and my different prisoner pits was supposed to also escort me to my death sentence, but he led me to an escape route instead. The hallway was... One I wish I could unsee. I ended up in a chute from one of the rooms that led me to the river. Zale, the guard, left me with the information to find the truck, and earlier this morning I did. After a bit of a brawl in Spokane, I came home as fast as I could. I owe The Elder and Zale my life."

Aiella stopped, more definitely this time, looking into the eyes of the loved ones in front of her. She exhaled a long breath, relief washing over her that she was now able to be an open book. She had gotten most of the important details out. The most exhausting day of her life thus far was almost over. It was a long few minutes before anyone spoke.

"How many others were there?" Alexis finally asked.

"A whole city-worth," Aiella replied. "Alongside the river there were shacks full of people, and up past the bank more was the looming city, with swarms of people at the execution. Beyond that, tucked into the side of the mountain, is where the fortress lies. I imagine Haydn's closest guards stay there. It is incredible and beautiful, but nothing good is inside it. I am guessing hundreds, maybe thousands, live there. Probably the former at this point," she concluded thoughtfully. She should have asked Zale some of these questions.

"I can't believe we are not the only ones," Luke said nervously.

"Ha," Aiella laughed dryly, "I've been considered naïve and self-absorbed for thinking that could ever be the case."

"Are they a threat?" Frank asked, his voice booming in comparison to the others.

"I don't know, honestly," Aiella sighed. "Lad, the one who I stole all of this stuff from, hinted that Haydn is the real threat, but that doesn't give me the most confidence that it's only him.

Lad said that there are many others. Of course, he tried to kill me, so I'm not sure how much I can trust any of what he said when I was buying myself some time," she corrected. "Master Haydn, though," she said slowly, "is another terrible story."

"How do you mean?" Frank asked tentatively.

"There are these weird abilities and power sources he has that I have never seen or heard of before, not until him." She looked desperately at him. Surely his engineering expertise would uncover what was going on.

"Like what?" Frank asked her slowly.

"This energy—it's like a glowing red light that can duplicate and be as powerful as it needs. Almost like it is living," she told him, pleading silently that he knew what it was.

"I don't think I have heard of anything like that either," he said with a frown. Aiella's heart sank. *This is just the beginning, isn't it?* She dropped her gaze. Gasping loudly, her hands met her face, her eyes on Alexis' finger.

"What is that!?" she exclaimed.

"Oh! It's—"

"I made it," Luke cut in proudly. "With some leftover metal that I found here and there on our broken appliances."

"And what exactly is it?" Aiella squealed.

"A promise ring!" Alexis blurted out excitedly. "We are going to be together forever," she added dreamily, gazing at Luke with cheeks flushed pink.

Luke ran his hand through his hair. "Lara was telling us about how they were prominent in the early 2000s, and we thought we would bring the trend back a century later. It seems silly now with all this going on…" His voice trailed off.

Aiella smiled. "Love is never silly. In fact, I think it's all we ever have." Frank looked at her with pride.

"Anyway!" Aiella breathed out loud, clapping her hands together. "We have a lot more to discuss! Getting off topic." She wanted to get this conversation over with so they could all move forward together. As she retold the rest of the story of being imprisoned, and seeing The Elder one last time, the mood in the room had changed drastically, and she found herself thankful for the millionth time that she had Luke and Alexis. They were only a few years younger than her, but they held onto this certain innocence in life, clinging to hope and love and all that was important, even when faced with adversity. They weren't naïve, either. They were both well-adjusted, intelligent young beings. But their curiosity, coupled with this invisible glow that emanated from them, kept everything in motion around here. Heck, they were the reason Aiella even wanted to find answers. Everything about them was inspiring, and she doubted they even knew it. Yet another thing that inspired her: how humble they each were. She felt overcome with the need to make the beautiful world outside livable for them. If anyone could heal it and make humanity flourish again, it was those two.

The room was silent.

"So, anyway…" Aiella said, yearning to go to sleep in an actual bed again, "That's what my week has been." Acting as though she was going to be ready for slumber, she watched as Alexis and Luke walked towards the kitchen and back to the quarters. Spinning back around, she was surprised to see Frank hadn't budged.

"You ready to fully tell me everything now?" he pushed, patting the seat next to him.

"How did you know?" She asked him quietly, staring at her folded hands in her lap.

"You seem too shaken up for that to be all," he answered plainly.

"I'm not shaken up," she started to protest. Frank merely raised an eyebrow. She sighed; this man was as close to a father as she would ever have. Of course, he knew there was more.

"I have been afraid to think about it, afraid that I was seeing things, afraid it is all a setup somehow. I was afraid to tell you this part of all things, but that hallway I escaped through... There was a spot that had my name on the wall." The fear that had been settling inside her for the past thirty or so hours came bubbling to the surface again.

"He's been looking for me, Frank," she whispered, the tears she was trying to hold back fighting their way out. "He's been searching for me for years, and I still can't understand why. My grandmother was torn from me, and Zale pulled away before I could ask the important questions."

"Oh, Ella," he muttered, pulling her head to his shoulder. "Shhh. It's okay. How do you know he has been looking for you anyway?"

"He made it obvious, for one," she sniffled, "and then the guard told me."

"Zale, right? Are you sure you can trust Zale?" he asked. Aiella nodded.

"My grandmother... She said to trust him. She confirmed it all."

"Okay," he said. "So what do we fully know about him? About Haydn?"

"Zale didn't just tell me to find the truck. He also told me to get the letter. As it turns out, this was hidden in the back of the truck. By the food." She managed to smile softly as she recalled his script relaying why it was in the food. Aiella placed the letter resting under her shirt into Frank's hands.

"What is this?" he questioned.

"As much as Zale could afford to explain to me. Haydn isn't from around here, and neither am I."

Chapter 19

T he night was restless for Aiella, much to her annoyance. Thinking she heard a few others flipping around in their sheets throughout the night didn't bring her as much comfort as it once did. She was exhausted mentally and physically, and the lack of rest was not doing her any good. Aiella wanted a fresh start. *Needed* a fresh start. She wanted to forget everything that had happened. But how could she? Not now, at least.

First thing in the morning, she slipped into the kitchen before anyone else was awake, unloading the food from her journey home into the small crates and cupboard niches dug into the walls. There wasn't much, but she knew everyone would be thankful for her return when they awoke today. She was sure the mood around here had been more depressing than usual in her absence, knowing Frank was likely inconsolable. She grabbed the loaves of bread and brought them close to her face to smell them. There was nothing like it, and she smiled in comfort at the opportunity to share this baked good with everyone shortly. She scurried around and found some dried berries they could eat with them and considered if she should leave for a couple of hours again just to bring them back a fish or two. They needed more protein and nutrients than what she could get them only two to three times per month. Perhaps it was time she started going out to gather provisions a few times a week instead. After being out and seeing the vast expanse of wild just in this small corner of their country, she was positive she would not be able to go without seeing it for more than a handful of days at a time.

"I see you haven't forgotten your way around here," Frank smiled, joining her in the small room.

"I wasn't gone that long," she replied with a laugh, breaking the loaves of bread into equal pieces for everyone to enjoy.

"Perhaps not, but it feels like you were," he said solemnly. "You seem to have grown into an adult overnight. I suppose I should say happy late birthday?" Frank smiled sadly.

"Are you saying I wasn't mature before?" She teased.

"No, at least not through your own fault. You just didn't have much of a reality check before, something you need to become fully responsible. Your eyes tell me you have seen a lot more than you can describe and have had a number done to your body that maybe you don't want to discuss. Your childhood innocence seems long gone now," he smiled sadly, "Bittersweet, really, watching your kid grow up."

Aiella finished the rationing and went to give him a hug, her heart swelling each time that he called her that. "You know you've always been like a father to me, and always will be," she reassured him.

"I'm worried about you, Ella," he frowned.

I'm worried about me, too, she thought. She wouldn't tell him that, though.

"It's unnecessary," she told him. "I am home, and will remain home. You don't need to worry. Since when are you so pessimistic, anyway?"

"When it involves you younglings," he said. "I don't think this is just something you can forget about. Nor do I think you should."

"Wasn't planning on it," she admitted. "I won't let The Elder's death be just another in Haydn's sinister plan - whatever it may be."

The eastern sector may be far, but over time she felt she could train herself to make it if needed. She had to find Satera. She did not dive into the details of hunger for the past few days with Frank, or tell him how she thought she was going to freeze to death. She had not told him about her guilt at leaving everyone else behind. It felt like their suffering was her fault, though she knew it couldn't be. Survivor's guilt, she guessed you could call it. She still hadn't told Frank about the strange crystal that had also saved her, the magic still resting on her chest. She also hadn't told him she had nearly died yesterday, the memory of her blood puddling around her as she gasped for precious air making her queasy. She wasn't lying to him, PerSay, but she was withholding a lot of truths. Her body twisted in conflict. It seemed like too much to explain last night, but now might be a good time to get the rest out.

"What are you not telling me still?" Frank urged, raising his voice slightly. She touched the stone underneath her shirt.

"We have a family here. To *protect*. Don't forget that." She heard herself say the last line and wondered if she really had changed in just a week. It was as though she went from viewing Frank as superior to a co-leader on the same level as her without even meaning to. Last night when she arrived, she had every intention of spilling all the tiny pieces out of her until she ran dry, but that would have only been helping herself. As she lay awake all night long, she realized just how much that was a selfish idea. She knew that everyone wanted to know the full details, but too much of them could harm them. Like Lad had said, anyone who went against Haydn ended up dead. Her goal had been to get back home and live her life protecting her family, and she had done half of that now. Aiella was the only one here who had seen everything out there. For the time being, she had to take sole responsibility for it all and formulate a plan.

Frank was shaking his head at her. "I can't believe you are acting so normal."

"After the week I have had, normal is what I need," she said coolly.

"I have a map, you know. A route for us to leave here."

"Wait, what?" She demanded. He just shrugged, patting his back pocket.

"Always safe with me, and ready. I think we might need it soon."

She heard others starting to wake up inside the sleeping quarters next to them and began counting out the dried berries for each inhabitant to go with the bread. She needed time to mull things over more. It all felt too strangely intimate. And dangerous. As everyone slipped in to grab their first meal of the day, giving "welcome back" greetings to Aiella, she slipped next door to the sleeping chambers. Eli passed her with a wistful glance before Alexis hugged her in passing, and she felt herself relaxing into a smile.

She walked to the far side of the room, where The Elder always found herself before, a melancholy chill passing through her. She sat down on the cot, bowing her head. Before long, Frank sat on the bed beside her with a sigh. Without speaking, she pulled the gem out from under her shirt. A strange energy was pulsating from it, tiny rainbows dancing onto the dirt ceiling above them.

"Incredible," Frank murmured, staring at it with an open mouth. "May I?" he asked, reaching a hand out cautiously.

"Mmhm," she muttered, watching him as his hand met the hard stone.

"This is the necklace that Zale mentioned in the letter to you, isn't it?" he asked her.

"Yes," she said softly. "Do you know what it is? I can't figure it out. I'm convinced it is what saved me, though. It's almost as though it senses me... senses what I need most. And then it helps me, gathering and transferring energy." *Like magic.*

"Ella," he said slowly, "I've never seen or heard of anything quite like this." Her heart sank.

"I imagine it must be from Satera, somewhere in the Eastern Sector..."

"I went there long ago. The Eastern Sector, I mean."

"And?" She raised an eyebrow, hope filling her.

"There was no Satera."

The light within her crushed. She had hit a dead end.

"This crystal," Frank continued in wonder, "there's nothing like it on Earth. Not that's known." Aiella stiffened.

The trees' pain. A disease that fantastically had people bursting into flame. A disease she knew Haydn had created. His powers... The stone. She thought maybe she had been injected as some kind of experiment as a baby, perhaps, but... No. Haydn wasn't from here. This planet. Which meant neither was Zale nor her grandmother...

Or her.

She should have known.

Gasping, she ran out of the chambers, past the kitchen and living room, and into the corridor leading to the outdoor world.

Aiella burst through the door in the ground and stepped up into the forest, inhaling the crisp morning air. A cyclone of wind and leaves swirled angrily around her. She wanted to run but had nowhere to go. On the flip side, staying was not a very viable option either. She was trapped. Again. Suffocated, hopeless, trapped as trapped can be. The air roared more viciously. Exhausted, she lay down on the damp ground, looking directly above her at a small opening in the trees. The earth was trembling beneath her gently, forcing her to take deep breaths. To concentrate. Why was nature so connected to her? Where was she from? *Who am I?*

This world was breathtaking.

Mother Nature was truly an artist. A few clouds were dancing across her line of sight to the sky, and she couldn't help but draw a smile at the outline of an animal on one. An elephant, perhaps, with a long trunk extending off of it. She looked to the left beside her and focused on a small blade of grass beginning to grow, even when the presence of pine needles should have overpowered it. A ladybug crawled slowly onto it and flew off on its next grand adventure as Aiella rolled over onto her side, taking long breaths. She ran her hand along the dirt, never having soaked up as much of her surroundings as she should have. She inhaled deeply through her nose, the smell of spring offering a plethora of emotions. It was a time for new beginnings, for rains to come and cleanse the past away.

She searched her mind for any insights she may have missed over the past couple of days. To Zale's forbidden, urgent kiss before she went tumbling into the river. To last night, her friendly embrace with Eli she was ashamed to admit left at least one of them wanting more. The look on Frank's face when she explained her story of the past week, the sparkle of hope in Alexis' eyes. Before going on her journey, Aiella thought she had a plan that would work everything out. She had a temper, she knew, but mostly because she always had something she knew was worth fighting for, though always small. She had tried being that obstinate person when she was under Haydn's watch, but something about him had broken her.

Could something that was broken turn into something stronger than ever before?

Hadyn's betrayal of the people he took responsibility for without even batting an eye, his sickening engrossment with her and her past, the way he enslaved humans for the benefit of only himself, thinking that he could make the world a better place by eradicating them... Everything about him was completely unethical, and everything about that city had broken her. She wondered what it was like around the rest of the world.

The rest of the universe, she reminded herself.

Eli sat down in front of her, interrupting her thoughts. The electricity she had felt between them last night was faded, but something else whirred deep within. She pulled the blade of grass out of the ground and looked at it, feeling numb and in need of a friend.

"You shouldn't be out here," she mumbled. She could feel his stare burning into her, making her blush.

"From the way you've been acting since you returned, something tells me the illness isn't the thing to be most worried about anymore." He cocked his head to the side, his eyes narrowing with a hint of a smile on his face. She contemplated that for a moment, her gaze still locked on the grass before her. Now that she knew Haydn was the one who had created the disease, and he had been searching for her all this time... Well, maybe it wasn't around anymore. He had found what he was looking for. She sighed, looking up at Eli patiently before her.

"There are others, aren't there?" Eli asked quietly. She gave a silent nod.

"Just like us?" he furthered. She hesitated, giving the smallest of shakes as her face cast itself downward. He didn't seem at all surprised by her responses.

"Did they hurt you?" Eli asked in a regretful undertone, concern leaking into his voice. This was a side of him she was seeing too often now. She sighed, wishing she had paid more attention around here over the past decade instead of floating through the motions she thought were correct.

"Yes," she told him quietly. Her eyes focused on the grass she was twirling around in her fingertips again. He nodded slowly as her body trembled. "Why does everyone know more about me than I do?" She pleaded, looking him in the eye finally, salty water threatened to burst. She blinked them away, speaking again before he could answer. "Never mind," she said, looking away and rubbing her arm across her face. She turned to face him again, and his expression was welcoming, sympathetic, and warm. Maybe he could run off with her.

Aiella sniffled. "It's just that... The ruler there has been searching for me. Neither of us is from here... not even remotely close! I haven't told Frank exactly what was in the lab, below where my name was," she whimpered, letting the tears fall. "It was for my execution specifically, and--"

"Shh, it's okay," Eli said, leaning over to wrap her in his arms.

"It's not," she sobbed. "He takes samples of people who enter Volcry, you know. What if he only created the disease to fish me out? And I'm the reason everyone suffers?" Aiella shook her head. Zale had said he did it as nobleness for the planet. "It's all too much to be a coincidence. And then The Elder tells me she's my grandmother? Plus, I'm not from Earth. And then she *dies?*" She cried out hysterically, her body not willing to stop now that it had begun.

"The Elder was your grandma?" He asked, pulling back in surprise, not even addressing the whole not-from-Earth part.

"Yes," she whispered. "Why is this all happening? What is going to happen to us all?" Aiella's face contorted in worry, mirroring Eli's as concern for both of their futures leaked out.

After a couple of minutes of silence, Eli tenderly placed his thumb under Aiella's jawline, chills making their way up her body from her toes. Her breath caught as he bent forward, his eyes shutting ever so slowly.

"I..." Aiella started breathlessly, turning up towards his lips.

"It's going to be alright, Ella," he whispered, leaning to close the gap between them.

Chapter 20

"I can't do this!" Aiella exclaimed, hopping onto her feet. Her fingers caressed her scalp, pulling on her hair as she started crying again.

"I'm so sorry, but I kissed someone else," she wept. "I kissed him. I can't do any of this without first knowing where my head is at. I can't..."

"It's beautiful out here," Eli breathed, looking around and cutting her off. "I had forgotten. It's been so long..."

"It is beautiful," she replied softly, confused by the lack of discussion of their almost-kiss. Confused but grateful.

Eli stood up beside her, a sad smile etched onto his mouth where a kiss should have been. "It's okay, you know. I understand. I'm here for you. And I can wait," he said with a wink.

"You are, without a doubt, my very best friend, Eli." Aiella grinned, wiping her eyes and shakily trying to stop herself from crying.

Suddenly, Aiella gasped, realizing something critical far too late.

"What's wrong?" Eli asked gently, his hand finding its way to her shoulder.

"I stole too much," she said in horror. The strange torch she had been using was obviously driven by Haydn's powers. How could she have been *so careless?*

"What? From who?" He pondered, joining her panic.

"Lad," she said, mostly to herself. "No, no, no, no, no! Oh, God, this can't be happening. He was too invested in getting me home." She was pacing again. "Something isn't right; I can feel it."

"What is happening? Who is Lad? If he's from that city, then he probably deserved to have things taken from him." Eli told her.

"He drove me to Spokane," she said, waving a hand before pulling on her scalp again. "Not knowingly. We fought, actually. I almost died..." She stopped, looking Eli square in the eyes. "He was supposed to bring me back to Haydn, but I managed to get away. But of course now they know that I must live around here. And Haydn knows I have people I care about with me. No, no, no..." She threw her hands in the air.

"I don't think I am following," Eli admitted.

"The strange light that I took. The torch and the smaller one... This man has tiny androids that drive cars. He's clearly apt in science, even aside from his more unusual abilities. He wouldn't let his workers go anywhere without being tracked. What if... What if it's tracked?" Aiella groaned loudly, covering her face with her hands. How could she let this happen? "He could even have my blood samples now, too." She shook her head. The puddle formed around her in the fight yesterday was enough to lap up into something.

"So?"

Aiella widened her eyes at him, speaking softly. "The tanks were filled with a strange liquid for my execution specifically. And the torch... It can't be from this planet. Not the essential components of it, at least." He looked at her blankly. "He had been telling his crew that they were going to find relatives of mine—that's what their mission was. Don't you see? Haydn knew about all of this somehow, I just know it... This was a backup plan of his all along. He probably wanted me to escape. To find all of you to use as leverage."

Her last sentence made Aiella's stomach flop. She felt uneasy during many parts of her trip home, thinking it was almost too easy to escape the fortress–with or without Zale's help. Yet she let herself go soft and accept the path. She put them all in danger. Stupid!

"We aren't safe," she said, looking all around them. There they were.

Her footsteps.

She never even thought twice about covering them up, and for all she knew they were trackable all the way back here from the city she brawled in.

"No," she gasped, putting her hand to her mouth and crouching down. She gestured for Eli to do the same.

"What are you doing?"

"Shh!" Aiella stood up to peek in the direction again.

Something was glowing in the woods. Something that looked bright and orange and... fiery and colorful like a sunset. It was nowhere close to evening. No, this was another light just like that on the torch that was now nestled down in the tunnels. Why would she trust taking anything that Haydn had to do with?

"We have to get the others and hide. Now!" Without wasting another second, they both hurried low to the ground to the door. Aiella tried to brush their footprints away and conceal them better with a branch on the ground, but she knew better. It wouldn't fool them. Not for long. Shutting the door overhead, she jumped down to the ground, not bothering with the ladder. There wasn't a moment to lose. Eli was already in the living room.

"Frank!" she yelled, sprinting in behind him. Everyone was in the main living den, staring at her.

Frank stood up, alarmed. "Wait, were you both outside?"

"I led them to us," Aiella admitted, her breath catching in her throat. Regret filled every cell of her body.

"Who?" he asked, concerned. But she knew he knew the answer.

"*Them*," she said emphatically, causing a stir around her. "We need to leave. Now. I hope you have that map ready, Frank."

Everyone stayed put in shock for a moment, not sure what to do or listen to. Finally, Frank grabbed a rolled piece of parchment from his pant pocket and yelled urgently.

"You heard her! Everyone up! Now! Go gather as much as you can carry and meet us out in the hallway!" Everyone remained frozen. "Do as you're told!" Frank yelled. "Your lives depend on it!" They all exchanged fearful looks, and then all hell broke loose.

As their familiar earthen walls seemed to crumble around them, Aiella's mind clouded. The shuffle of panic around her deafened as a woman's voice, probably Alta's, whispered, "Where will we go?" to Frank. Another hand tugged on her arm.

"Ella, what do we do?" Dimitri asked urgently, Lara holding his hand beside him. She desperately looked around for Luke and Alexis, finding them clinging tight to each other against the far wall, their few belongings draped over them. Some of the stronger men were trying to carry out the larger items from the kitchen.

"There is another tunnel. An escape route. Frank and I have been sure to keep it livable over the years, and there is a contraption built to lock us all inside there, nearly impossible for anyone to get through." Her voice strengthened as she kept talking; they were all going to be okay. They had expected this, no matter how lightly, for the last decade at least. That's why there was an escape route to begin with. They nodded, and scurried off with the others, stuffing their arms full of pillows and food, with eyes full of fear.

Frank came running back into the living area as well, carrying as much from the kitchen as anyone possibly could with the help of Darian. Food could be easily replaced, but these appliances could not. "All right, all who are ready, follow me!" He shouted over the chaos, leading a handful of them into the outer tunnel. Aiella watched them all go, still rooted to the same spot she had been.

This is all my fault, she told herself, watching with distress as her family, one by one, dashed with all the belongings they could out of the home that had kept them safe for years. She wanted to crawl into a hole, one deeper than the tunnel, and disappear. *All my fault.* The remaining people of the tribe were knocking into her, but she didn't care. Why had she come back home at all? She had led threats directly to them. Her feet were rooted to the ground. She knew that she could not go with everyone to safety. They were coming here for Aiella. She mindlessly made her way towards the trapdoor, prepared to offer herself up.

"Ella!" She looked behind her, Eli and Frank running towards her. She put a finger to her lips and pointed up.

"They're here," she whispered. "They're here, and it's all my fault."

"Ella, we don't have time for that. We have to go now. We can get to safety and barricade ourselves!" Eli's voice was breaking. He knew she had no intention of joining them. She gave him the same sad smile he had shared with her only minutes before. "Please," he whimpered, "don't stay here." She simply shook her head. "Ella," he said, closing the rest of the distance between them. He embraced her in a hug. "I'll stay, too." Before she could object, Frank stepped in.

"You won't," he told him firmly. "It's time for you to go, boy. You're in charge now." He handed the map over to him, along with something that Aiella couldn't make out, her eyes fogging up with tears.

"Alexis and Luke," she said sadly, her heart breaking. They were already gone. Surely they expected her to be right behind. "Tell them I love them, and that they are the future." Tears poured down her face, but she saw Eli give a curt nod. She ran to him through blurred vision, taking his face in her hands. "I will see you again," she promised, her voice quivering as the surrounding ground started to ever so slightly tremble.

"You will," he confirmed. "Soon." Tears trickled down his face, too, as he kissed her on the cheek. After one last quick hug, he left reluctantly, looking back at them as she wiped her face.

"What have I done, Frank?" She asked, her voice caught in her throat.

"Nothing," he said quietly.

"Is there anything left to grab?" She asked, a thud landing on the door to the outside world above them. She covered her head as specks of dirt fell. His eyes were glistening as though in a trance. "Frank," she persisted. That door would open any minute now. "You have to go; they want me!" He nodded, taking off in the direction of the others. The trapdoor above her flew open. She fled towards the living area as a large crumbling noise shook the air from the direction everyone had fled. Aiella let out a sigh of relief. The others were safe and barricaded.

Running into the kitchen, Aiella crouched behind a counter in the corner. The earth was dug out curiously here, a fun spot to play hide and seek when she was younger. Oh, how she longed for those times. It was a tight squeeze, and she had been a master at hiding. She hoped they wouldn't find her here, at least until she figured out her plan of attack.

She heard footsteps enter the room. More than one person had come.

"Well, well." Her stomach dropped. *Master Haydn himself.* "It would appear she did have a family," he said to the others, kicking over a chair. "Nicely done, Lad. Though I wonder where could they have gone?" Aiella wanted to cry. So she had been right. She led them straight here. *The last time I don't follow my gut.* How could anyone set up their entire family for its demise?

Chapter 21

"I told you all I know, Master! The torch was brought here; you tracked it yourself! You have her blood now, too, thanks to my knife wound. She must have caught on and gone with them, but I held up my end of the--"

"Oh stop, Lad!" It was Zale's voice coming this time. Aiella shivered in her corner. Had he betrayed her as well? Her entire body shook at the thought. She tried to reason with herself that it was the only way to save his life.

"Can you two *both* shut up!" Haydn barked. "Treason and betrayal to me. That is what your sentence will be if you do not help. Acting like it was a bloody accident, she got away!" He screamed, and Aiella could picture the spit flying out of his mouth in anger. "If I don't get to kill *her*, I will kill *you*," he added with a growl. "The agreement was to bring her to me after trying to get out of her where her family was. You failed. It's that simple." Aiella swallowed, tears in suspense on her eyelids.

"At your service," Zale bowed. When he bent over, he got low enough to see Aiella, their eyes meeting ever so briefly. He cleared his throat, standing straight again.

"What did she do to deserve this?" Lad asked. *Why ask that? Was there decency inside of him?* Aiella remembered the look on his face when he spoke of Aggie being executed. Had he opened up to anyone else like that before? It wasn't like he thought she could tell anyone his secrets. *Shut up,* Aiella pleaded silently to him. *He's going to kill you. Shut up!*

Haydn started laughing.

"What did she *DO*?" He chuckled more deeply, an eerie wave of emotions soaking through the tunnels. The sound of flesh being ripped and a body slamming the ground bit into her, tears falling rapidly into her lap.

"No!" Zale screamed. Aiella covered her ears, willing the world to go away. Still, she stayed rooted.

"Ella!" A voice called out.

Frank.

No. No, no, no! Aiella began sobbing silently. She wasn't in a position to save him right now. She was fine hiding here, and on the other side of that curtain, he no longer was. Why did he come after her? He should have fled with the others. Or left and waited outside the trapdoor. *Please not Frank. NO!* she prayed. She peeked out from behind her hiding spot, seeing Lad's body crumpled on the floor. She covered her mouth with her hand, twisting back around and wishing she had a cloth to bite down on. *He died because of me.* Blood gushed out of his neck, a huge gash glistening in crimson across it, the edges looking singed. She closed her eyes, trying to make the image go away.

It stayed.

From her place in the shadows, she saw Haydn's face contort in glee. He walked back into the living area.

Zale looked down at Lad, water dripping down one cheek, just a single tear, as he crouched and looked at Aiella again. He gave a slight shake of his head, then stood up straight again, following Haydn into the room.

Aiella silently climbed out of her concealed spot in the corner, abandoning her safety with it. *Haydn doesn't know I am here,* she reasoned. She knew Zale was trying to warn her not to try to play hero. Terror burst into her, though, as she realized they would kill everyone in their way until she was found. *Found or known to be elsewhere,* she realized. She didn't want Frank to become what Lad was below her, his blood draining into the dirt floors. His eyes widened in shock.

"I'm so sorry," she whimpered quietly to him, though she didn't expect him to hear. She made her way slowly to the entrance of the living room. *This ends now,* she thought. She inhaled a deep breath and grabbed the curtain with a shaking hand. Frank speaking made her freeze.

"You're the monster she told me about," Frank said to Haydn. "You killed our friend. Ella's grandmother!"

"Not just her grandmother," he said, too much glee dripping from his voice. "Her parents too."

"How could you cause so much pain to people? How do you live with yourself?"

"I loved Ella's mother and treated her well. Or so I thought! She could have joined my cause. She could have chosen me! Her death was her own doing," he said coolly. "Aiella was offered the same opportunity. To join me. She refused it."

Aiella stiffened at the mention of her name. She didn't hear a response from Frank, making her afraid of what she couldn't see. Now was her chance...

"Where is she now?" Haydn demanded. More silence. *Just give me up and save yourself, Frank,* she pleaded to him with everything in her.

As though he had heard her, he whispered, "I would never sacrifice you for me." *Could she manipulate thoughts?* What difference was there between her and Haydn if she manipulated others just as he did? Volcry was filled with unwilling people he had created into slaved monsters, out to destroy everything they once held dear.

Haydn let out a surprising cackle, hands clapping together. "A-ha! She is still here, isn't she?"

"No!" Frank insisted, perhaps too hastily. Aiella stumbled backward, trying to find somewhere to hide. As she curled up in the same earthy corner as before, Haydn came barging through the curtains into the kitchen, searching fervently for her.

"Nowhere to hide. We were just here," Zale said, walking into the other room again. Aiella saw Haydn throw up his hands, walking belligerently into the sleeping quarters behind him. She let out her breath, ready to get up as Frank came propelling into the room, finding her instantly.

"You leave. Now," he whispered rapidly.

"You too," she hissed.

"They'll notice you're not back there within a minute. That's not enough of a head start. I'll hold them off." He spoke firmly.

"No!" Her heart sank. She couldn't leave the closest thing she had to a father. She couldn't. She wouldn't. "We can figure it out together," she said, standing up. She grabbed his arm, trying to quietly pull him with her.

"None of this was your fault, Ella," he said near-inaudibly.

"It is, though," she replied sadly. They needed to go. There were only so many rooms to search. She tilted her head towards the living area, and Frank followed her out silently, glancing behind them.

"Ella, listen to me." He held her close for a moment. His eyes glossed over, the voices behind them getting louder again.

"Frank, no," she begged.

"It will be okay." He took a step back, his finger to his lips, Haydn and Zale in just the room next door.

The ground began to shake violently.

"No," Aiella whispered, though her body began stepping away. Before Frank could say anything back, Haydn walked through the curtain.

"There you are," he said, pleased.

"Leave!" Frank yelled at her. She turned towards the exit, the earth around her beginning to come down in slivered pieces. She covered her head, mere steps away from the curtain that led to the trapdoor.

"Aiella! You can't hide from me!" Haydn shouted over the sound of the earthquake. Aiella spun back around, horror gripping every cell in her body as she saw the fire sitting on his palm. He smirked through the dust. "You're more powerful than you know. Don't you feel it?" She looked around her, larger pieces of the ceiling beginning to crash down. "Now is your last chance," Haydn continued to yell. "Join me! Together, we can rebuild a society our people and planet deserve!"

"No!" Aiella cried. Haydn turned his hand sideways, with a blue and orange flame contained on top of it. She looked at Zale, who helplessly shook his head. With a twist of his arm, the flame met Frank, his voice wailing out in pain.

"NO!" she screamed again, the earthquake becoming more ferocious. Larger bits of sediment began falling, the sofa on which she had shared so many memories becoming crushed by a huge rock that must have been suspended in their ceiling. She saw Frank's body contorting. The furniture next to him caught fire as well. Dirt shot around everywhere, making it impossible to see.

A hand pushed her in the chaos, the grumbling earth not stopping. "Go!" Zale urged her, forcing her through the curtains to leave, throwing another body behind her. Instinct overtook her, and she ran, grabbing Frank's arm and forcing him to follow. She shoved him in front of her, hearing Haydn's screams to Zale as she grabbed the cool metal.

"She's going to get away!" Zale was coughing in the distance. Smoke filled the corridor. They scrambled up the ladder to the outside world as her home was filled with thick ash and rock. As they climbed out into the fresh air, the cliff threatened to collapse beneath her feet.

"There!" Aiella yelled, pointing to a large boulder a few yards away. Frank struggled over without question to help drag it over the door.

"That won't hold long, but it'll give us a chance," he panted. His stamina was already not as good as hers, and she feared he wouldn't make it far. As if reading her mind, he solemnly added, "Ella, if it comes to it, you must leave me behind."

"What did he do to you?"

She shook her head exasperated, tearing off part of her shirt and placing it in bark in the opposite direction of where they were going. *How does he look unscathed? What just happened?*

"What's that for?" Frank questioned.

"Get them started on the wrong track, even if briefly," she said breathlessly. If they survived. *If.* She was torn, wanting Haydn dead, but Zale alive. She had a feeling she wouldn't get both. With tears still streaming down her face, she took off sprinting. "In case they make it out alive, we can't lead them in the direction of the others." Without objection, Frank took off breathlessly beside her, clutching his chest now and then. As they got further away, Aiella was relieved to not hear anyone trailing close behind them, thanking the sky that their stalls must have worked.

"The earthquake," she said, heaving heavily. "Why did Haydn think it was me?" She paused, wheezing to catch her breath while on the run.

"Maybe it was?" Frank said as he shrugged, too focused on gasping, trying to suck in air, to seem to think too hard about it.

"Maybe..." *But how?*

They kept running deeper into the unknown.

Night was hitting before they allowed themselves to slow their pace.

"I can't believe I was only back for one night," Aiella muttered.

"You and me both, kid," Frank said with a sigh.

"We're sure the others are okay, right?" She asked tentatively.

"Yes," he said in a low voice.

"We need to build or find shelter," she spoke after a long pause. "It's getting dark." She looked overhead at the blackening sky, missing the tunnels. The tunnels that burned further into the ground...

"And... We should talk about what happened." Aiella sighed. They had been avoiding any type of discussion for the past few hours, but now she thought it might ironically ease the tension. Now that they had completely slowed to a walk in search of somewhere to rest, the timing was impeccable. Her thoughts were met with silence.

"Frank," she ushered. He nodded his head thoughtfully.

"What do we discuss first?" He whispered with a chuckle, walking around them to scan for somewhere to camp for the night.

"Do you think they escaped?" she asked.

"I do." She felt an invisible weight being lifted off her, both fearing and hopeful he was right. She couldn't bear to think that Zale had died at her hands. But this meant that they were likely being chased, and for how long they would search, she couldn't say. Haydn had been looking for her this long, after all.

Her heart broke thinking of Lad dying in her home. Haydn murdered him without even batting an eye. Lad did terrible things, but fire couldn't be put out with fire. *Hadyn killed him, just like her grandmother.* She couldn't believe she had lived these years not knowing of the blood relation to the one who had saved her and brought her to her family here. She couldn't believe Haydn could ruthlessly kill those he took under his wing for years. What drove him to be so evil? Was it somehow her?

"It wasn't your fault," Frank reflected, pointing to an opening ahead. "Come on, there's a small cave over here. It looks like. Light the torch."

Aiella took a few minutes failing to light the torch she had been working at making as they journeyed. Everything from her trip to the city had been left behind, likely now perished forever. Everything except the letter and necklace from Zale, which she had clung to her skin for dear life. An idea sparked in her mind, and she removed the glowing stone from under her shirt, focusing on the colors dancing off of it. She imagined them dancing in the torch.

A surge of energy flowed out through her into the crystal, licking her veins and shooting blue sparks, like small fireflies in the night, onto the end of the stick. A smile filled her face, a beautiful light now shining the way for them. Frank raised an eyebrow with a grin, clearly impressed.

"What's this newfound ability?" He asked her.

"I have no idea, but I like it," she said with a smile.

Chapter 22

They cautiously approached the opening of the shallow cave together, relieved when they found no sign of wildlife hiding within it. Once huddled inside, Frank pulled out a canteen of water from his sagging back pocket for them to sip.

"At least I didn't wind up fully empty-handed," he boasted. She held off diminishing the torch's glow, hoping that would trap some heat inside the cave for a while.

"It wasn't your fault. None of this is your fault," Frank told her again, lying down on the ground.

"It feels like it," Aiella replied miserably, trying to concentrate on the swirling blue flames. "If I had not left and gone looking for answers, Lad would not have been put in the position he was. Maybe The Elder would have gotten away, completing her mission without interference. I wouldn't have been followed. Our home would not have been destroyed..." She imagined she should be crying but felt hollow.

"Your grandma..." Frank mumbled. More to himself, he added, "I shouldn't have let secrets and limits run our lives for so many years." He sounded just as ashamed as she felt guilty. They both gave out a depressed sigh. "Ella..." Frank started again. "I know it's hard, but please listen to me right now." He turned to face her, sitting up again so he could better look at her face. She glanced at his eyes, seeing for her troubles reflected back at her.

"The world has always had problems and corruptions. You were not the one who did that. You were so young when the outbreak happened. I bet you can't remember anything prior to it, especially not the bad. But it was there. It's always been there. Humans are frail, and we make a lot of mistakes. Sometimes I think the mistakes, almost always driven by emotion, are what make us who we are." He paused.

"He killed my parents, Frank," she said softly. "He killed everyone. And with these powers, this magical light-filled necklace... It is more clear than ever that Satera is far, far away."

"And to think you've been ashamed that you ever left." Frank soberly voiced his input.

"My dear Ella, you learning about yourself is amazing. It's not something to be ashamed of. You may not have accomplished what you wanted to, but this might be the start of answers that the entire world has been in search of."

"I don't know who I am," she trembled, "And I fear that you will be hunted next. How can I help the world find answers when I don't even have answers about myself?" Her words suspended like cold fog in the air.

"You're the same person you have always been," he reassured her.

"I never even knew I needed to ask questions about myself. I don't know if I'm enough to help those I care about." She hung her head.

"You'll always be enough," he smiled. "I am proud to call you my daughter." She lay down on the ground now, taking deep breaths and holding them in. She counted to five before she allowed herself to release. It helped her quiver less, calming her, though she noticed the crystal was starting to burn even brighter.

"What is going on with Eli and you?" He smirked as he spoke. "Can't help but notice he was outside with you before..." His voice trailed off as he cleared his throat.

"*Was*," she emphasized. "Past tense. And nothing anyway. We are best friends."

"Right," he chuckled. Aiella glared at him, turning over to attempt to put out the torch.

"For your information, I kissed Zale. The guard."

"What?" Frank roared with laughter. When Aiella raised an eyebrow at him, he quickly stopped. "You're kidding? That's blasphemy." He gave a low chuckle. "No wonder he helped save us." He laughed hard for a moment - the situation was pretty unbelievable.

"So, tell me more about the world before it had the catastrophe that is me," she changed the topic.

Frank lay down beside her. "It wasn't entirely screwed up," he started. Aiella shot him a scolding look, Frank getting the hint that this was supposed to be something to make her feel better. "Though it was a mess," he admitted, "you aren't the first one to feel like the weight of the world is on your shoulders, and with any luck you won't be the last." The fire's lingering ember went out, enveloping them both in total darkness, the cave above them blocking out the stars. Aiella wondered where the moon was tonight, then accepted it must be in a darker phase as well. Something about the moon comforted her.

Frank continued, "To tell you the truth, throughout the history of humanity we've made a lot of mistakes as a species. Some big, some more insignificant. All of them mattered, and yet didn't matter at all." Aiella pondered that for a moment, knowing the truth behind it. Frank had taught her about science from a young age. She knew that the planet was over four and a half billion years old, and the universe a few times that. With the average lifespan in the 22nd century - before the outbreak, at least - being ninety-seven, it didn't take a math-whiz to realize that the life of a single human amounted to very little in comparison to the existence of the universe, of the planet, of even the time humans had been evolving and growing and passing on more knowledge.

Frank had once said that the purpose of life was theorized by many to be the passing on of knowledge to each new generation. He said that when you look at any problem, and then look at the night sky, all of it seems infinitesimal. The theory sounded more like a way for people not to lose their mind wondering what their purpose was. Wasn't that always the question? Her mind was derailing, and all in half a second. She shut her eyes and took a deep breath again, focusing on Frank's stories.

"There have been genocides of people, some because of religion, others because of someone's appearance. Still more were because a select few were greedy and wanted power. They didn't know how to take "no" for an answer and sought out any method they felt they needed to in order to get that answer to turn to "yes." Sometimes this led to war, or simply the killing off of large groups of innocent people." Aiella shivered, feeling like she was in the midst of living through exactly that. How strange to be living through a revolution. As though you are the words in a textbook.

"I like to see the good in people, because I truly believe that when a person is born, they are inherently good. The world is what changes them. It breaks them at times, making them gain a less than desirable perspective. But the latter is humans making excuses. That's another flaw many for as long as we have existed have had: the lack of accountability. We force blame onto each other and our surroundings, not wanting to believe that we make mistakes. But humans do. We make mistakes. Nothing is perfect. Not in nature, not in the universe, so certainly not in humans. I think if there is a God, he sneezed when he was making us. Or, perhaps he wanted us to grow to be more beautiful than we could imagine by embracing the good with an appreciation born out of the mishaps. The darkness. There historically has been so much darkness... That's not just now. This is not a first." She stared up at the dark ceiling of the cave, feeling one with it. He continued.

"When the outbreak occurred, had the world been more communicative and joined together instead of becoming more segregated over the years as it had, we might have stood a chance." His voice fluttered off for a moment, as if deep in thought, wondering how different the world may have been now. "But we were divided. And humans weren't the only ones we hurt through it all. The environment was failing in the second half of the twenty-first century. Thousands of species went extinct. Being an engineer, I was always looking for ways to be more eco-aware, but others didn't care about that. Only about saving time and money. Corruption has always been prevalent."

"That sounds terrible," Aiella mumbled. "Maybe some loss was for the best."

"No," Frank whispered. Aiella thought she might be hearing him sniffling. "Humans have their flaws, but the majority are good people. So many good people. With good intentions. The fine line between love and hate was just always being blurred..."

"I'm sorry," she told him solemnly, "I realize how insensitive that must have sounded. It's just that everything you describe makes it sound like being alive means endless suffering. Forever. I don't know if I have the energy to make it another eighty or more years like this." She ran her fingers mindlessly along the crevices of the crystal around her neck. *80 years.* She didn't even know if she would be around for the next 80 days.

"Ella?" He spoke more softly, gaining her attention even more. "There is, was, and always will be, more good than evil." He let the words sink in. She did not understand how he could genuinely think that. How could he think there was good in the world when he lost his wife and child? How could he think that light outweighed all the dark when people were enslaving each other, destroying one another and their surroundings, and life was something so fragile?

"Remember that for me, okay?" He persisted. She gave a slight nod, but he couldn't see it. "Think of Luke and Alexis. That ring he made her." She felt him looking her way through the dark. "Love is the most powerful thing on the planet, no matter what anyone else thinks. It's all that matters. And it always prevails. Even when evil tries to snuff it out, it is always there. Nothing can break it, not permanently." His voice softened. "I would live my life with my wife and kid over and over again, even knowing the outcome. I would go through that suffering any day if it meant one more second with them. That has to stand for something. When everything else seems so insignificant, it has to mean something. We are here for a reason, every single one of us. Some of us just never get the opportunity to find out why."

They lay in silence for a few minutes, Aiella trying to analyze what he had just told her in the present context. She wasn't sure if it was her exhaustion, lack of answers, or his eloquent and emotional talk that made her figure it out, but she made a vow to herself right then and there. She was going to find out all she could about herself, and she was going to help as many as possible. Her family, the people in the broken city, and any others that were divided, or otherwise incapacitated, by life. Every single person left had gone through something terrible. Something people before them only thought of in their wildest nightmares. She knew the worst was likely still to come, but she also knew she would not give up. She knew she wouldn't be able to help every soul, but she still had to try. She would not cave to the bad in the world. She wouldn't cave to Haydn. She breathed through her nose, inhaling the crispest air, and let the glow of her necklace warm her. Curling up, she was surprisingly at ease. It was terrifying to think what was next, but for once she knew the direction she was headed in. For once, she had a solid purpose.

"I'm going to save us all, Frank," she muttered with confidence as she began to drift off. With Frank by her side, believing in her, anything was possible.

"You're the only one who can, Ella," she heard him gently said. And then sleep overcame her.

A few hours passed as she drifted in and out of dreams, finally hearing Frank moan loudly, the sky still dark outside the cave.

"Hmm? What is it?" She asked sluggishly, holding tighter to her necklace as she rolled over the other way.

"Something is wrong," he moaned deeper, her eyes flashing open as she sat up.

"What? What's wrong?" She asked frantically, her gaze immediately trailing outside the cave. "Is someone out there?" She whispered. She cursed herself for ever having fallen asleep.

"No," Frank replied softly.

"What?" she quipped. "What's wrong then?" She crawled over to where he was sitting against the cave wall. His hand was gripping his chest.

"It burns," he cried, clawing at his neck. *Haydn.*

"What do you mean it burns? Where? You look okay." She wasn't sure if she was attempting to reassure him or her.

"Inside. I think he gave it to me."

"Gave what to you?" She inquired, worry setting into her stomach, the palms of her hands sweaty. But she already knew. The flame he had touched Frank with in the tunnels. The sickening blue and orange coil of fire. It was too good to be true that they escaped unscathed.

"You already know," he winced. "We have to get moving," he insisted. "I don't know how long we were asleep."

"It's still dark," she muttered. How would they move anywhere if he was suffering in pain as he was? She didn't budge from her spot next to him.

"You can't save the world inside this cave," he persisted. "I will be fine." His grimacing face told her otherwise. Her heart felt like it was falling through the ground, the world around her seeming colder. Frank had ceremotosis, meaning their days together were limited. When had it started? In the night, or the minute it touched him, slowly eating away at him this whole time?

"Come on," he said, breathing through the pain with a groan. "It's just about twilight. We'll get a colorful show if we head out now." Aiella just stared at his figure in the shadows, trusting the person who had taught her everything she knew. Trying not to let his impending doom ruin the time she had left with him.

"I can't let you die," she whispered. She cried quietly, wrapping her arms around him as tight as she could. "There has to be a way

I can help you. There has to." She buried her face in his shirt, never wanting to leave the comfort. She couldn't let Frank die. She couldn't fathom not seeing again. Not when they had made it this far. "No," she whimpered. The ground began to shake.

"Another earthquake?" Frank pondered, pulling back to wipe off her face. "Come on, Ella. It's time to go." She shook her head, but inhaled a deep breath, anyway. The earth stopped shaking. *Maybe it was her.* Her body was numb as they stepped out of the cave together. It wasn't time to mourn yet.

"Why must everything be falling apart?" She murmured. "I can't do this alone. I had a plan. I'm supposed to help everyone, but how can I without..." She couldn't say it. Frank returned a sigh, limping beside her. In the dim twilight, she could already see burn marks forming all over his body, the tips of his fingers a charred black. She shuddered, too small to have remembered what this suffering looked like. His family had gone through this. The whole country, the whole world, had suffered through this. Already the damage was more irreparable than what the citizens of Volcry had sustained. He didn't have as much time as she even had thought, small flames now beginning to force holes through his shirt and pants. Tears dripped down her face, turning towards the rising dawn.

"It's beautiful, isn't it?" He whispered with a cough.

"It is," she said, wiping her face with her sleeve and reaching for his hand. "Ouch!" She yelped, flinching. He gave her a sad smile, turning away to continue walking. Not even twenty minutes later, he stumbled onto the ground.

"He accelerated it faster," he breathed, curling up on the ground. The surrounding leaves sparked into flames as fire rolled off of him.

"Frank!" Aiella cried, kneeling down beside him.

"Please, Ella," he whispered, "I want to watch you walk away in the golden hour of the sun, and I want to live my last moments taking in nature in solitude." He broke into a fit of coughs, blood spurting from his lips. He wiped it aside, his hands now entirely burned. "I used to take my family camping in places like this..." He fell to his back, looking up at her with pleading eyes. "Hopefully, it won't be too long until I rejoin them."

Aiella's head was spinning, the world around her crumbling apart more, but she found herself nodding in agreement. She felt like she was watching her body from afar, the thought of being entirely alone in this world completely overwhelming. She couldn't go back to try to find her family, she didn't even know where to start. Besides, that would only put them in more danger. She had made the decision to go the opposite direction, and thank the planet for that! Was Haydn's plan all along to infect every one of them besides her? Leaving her to watch them perish within the same day?

Frank was going to die, and it was entirely because of her. That was inevitable. Eli would protect the others.

Being as gentle as she could, she scurried to a thick ball of moss, rushing it back to him to put his head on top. He burned to the touch, his skin slowly melting away.

"I don't want you to see me fully succumb," he told her, his eyes the only thing not afflicted. "And the flames... they'll tell them where we are. I imagine that was his plan all along." Aiella shook her head, still refusing to believe what was happening. She bitterly wished that Haydn could see he had failed to at least some extent, Frank never spreading it to the others.

"I can't leave you," she whimpered. "What do I do? I can't do this all alone."

"You are so much more capable than you believe you are," he managed to gasp. "Today is the first day of a better future," Frank reminded her. She could see his breathing slowing. Her throat ached from the sobs trapped inside her.

"Hard to believe that could be the case, considering you won't be in it. I need you," she wept, tears sweeping off of her onto the ground below them.

"Our happiness is the only thing we are truly in control of, Ella," he exhaled. She nodded, the sobs growing in her chest, tumbling out.

"I will do everything I can," she promised through her tears. "I will do everything in my power to grow, to learn, and to help the people and society of the future. For you," she sobbed. Frank weakly pulled her into his fatherly embrace. Pain ripped through her entire being, but she clung tight to him. Her tears caused sizzling sounds to erupt as they landed on his skin, and for a moment she expected them to heal him. An awful spell would be broken. But this was no fairytale.

"Shh... Shh. Now, now, it will be alright." He pushed her off of him, her shirt now filled with holes and burn marks. She looked behind his face, seeing the light from the sun rising up. His eyes pierced her soul, and she willed him to know how much she loved him. She shut her eyes, weeping inconsolably. This was happening too fast. It was too unfair. She opened her eyes, the crystal around her glowing black.

"I'll always be here," he groaned. He put his hand over his heart, and she did the same. "In your heart. You are never alone." He smiled weakly. "Now, go. Please." She stood up, feeling her world slipping away from her.

"You are more than your struggles, and everyone has them," he whispered. She stared at him, her vision blurring. "Remember that..." She nodded, understanding, tears pooling between them.

"Don't go," she sobbed helplessly. The sun was coming through the trees, a breathtaking gold color that only the universe and its magic could create.

"It's time... My dear Ella."

Tears ran down her face as she got up and gathered her belongings. She looked at Frank, writhing in pain on the earth. "I love you, Dad," she whispered. She didn't get a response. She turned away, the image of him still trying to smile with fondness at her forever burning into her mind. She took off sprinting, not daring to look back. With her vision muddled with teardrops, her sorrowful howls echoed off the branches of the forest as flowers sprouted up around Frank's perishing body.

Chapter 23

How? The single-word question that had been gnawing away at her for two days now. *Has it been that long already?* Had she slept?

Her arms burned, her legs burned, her back burned. Cuts and bruises covered most of her bottom half, the result of stumbling and falling countless times as she wept. The earth kept rumbling beneath her steps, branches lashing out and whipping her limbs. She didn't know which direction was which anymore. She didn't care about the pain. How would she live with herself? How would she continue on? How could she hope to help or protect anyone?

Eventually, she knew that she would collapse. And she didn't mind that idea. *No*, she hadn't slept. Not that she could decipher, anyway. The world and her nightmares were now one. Trying to differentiate them was pointless. So she ran, waiting for her body to give out. Praying it would give out.

Running forced her to calm down and find rhythm to her breathing, though. Grounding her. The shaking slowly stopped. The physical pain started to take precedence. Every now and then she still choked on sobs that escaped sporadically, but the numbness of trying to block everything out and give up could only last for so long. She didn't have any clue as to where she was going. Everything burned inside of her. It reminded her of fire. And smoke. And the smell of Frank's sizzling corpse...

She ran some more.

Then, when she thought she didn't have the strength to keep going, she ran faster.

The events of the past couple of weeks zipped through her mind as though they were racing against a mountain lion. Her legs met the rise and fall of the earth beneath her, but her mind was hovering somewhere unknown. Zale wasn't from Earth, and neither was her grandmother. Or Haydn. *Or her.*

Where was she from? Where this place called Satera was, she had no clue. How she was going to ever get there? Not even the faintest idea. Would she ever stop causing destruction and pain? Again, no idea.

What made her different from Haydn? Did it matter if your intentions were good or bad if you still hurt the people you cared about? Frank would have told her yes. But he wasn't here. Because of her.

"Aaahh!" She screamed up to the air, clutching her fingernails so deep into her hair and scalp that she felt them get warm with oozing liquid. The blood at her temples threatened to burst out;

her legs wobbled unsteadily beneath her. Her lungs burned, trying to take in as much air as they could, but to little avail. Finally, her body demanded she rest.

The ground greeted her knees with a hard thud as her body crumpled onto its side, everything a dizzying slow motion. She rested her head on the cool dirt, shouting in pain - whether emotional or physical she no longer knew or cared - as her screams turned into heavy sobs.

"I'm sorry, Frank," she wept, curling her knees into her chest. She bit her knuckle, rocking her body back and forth on the forest floor. "I'm so sorry, Dad," she wailed. "I know I said I would try for you, but I don't know if I can."

For the first time in well over twenty-four hours, not that she had kept track, she allowed herself to mourn without running away. Her wails echoed off the trees, scattering birds into the air. At this point, it didn't even matter to her if Haydn was to survive and find her. Anything would be better than this. Her eyes swollen from tears, she finally dozed off.

Chapter 24

Haydn.

Aiella awoke abruptly, sweating as her eyes flashed open to the pitch black forest. A cool breeze passed over her, bringing with it the hoot of an owl off in the distance. Concentrating on the crystal she wore, willing it to emanate light, she was amazed to see that within moments brightness did in fact dance off of it. It seemed she was capable of more than she knew. Just like Haydn thought.

Haydn.

Gritting her teeth, she jumped to her feet, her skin crawling. Had he survived?

She paced, her fingers at her temple once again. She couldn't give up now. She couldn't succumb to what had happened. *That's what Haydn wanted.* Her nightmare reminded her of that. There were still people on Earth whom she loved. Alexis, Luke, and Eli, to name a few. There were people worth fighting for. Even if that meant facing her dark truths every day.

She sat down on an old stump overgrown with her favorite moss, the stone around her neck illuminating just enough of it to see the vibrant green coloring. She leaned her face against her hands with a tired sigh, cringing when she touched the crusty edges of her hair. *Burned.* Singed from the last hug she would ever give Frank. Another whimper escaped her, the crystal beginning to glow more of a brilliant, smooth black again instead of soft greens as it had been moments before. Like a collapsing star had been turned into something she could wear. She knew it was reflecting what she could feel.

Groaning, she bent forward and placed her head between her knees. She had not paid any mind to the extent of how exhausted she was since she lost her family, and she regretted it now. She needed water. She needed to survive if she was going to save anyone. It would be impossible to hunt or gather in the dead of night, so she curled up next to the stump, the dampness around it oddly comforting. It was like the forest was mourning with her, too.

She spent the next morning focused solely on her longevity, a task that proved easier said than done. Though she had keen survival skills, she was nowhere near fresh water, and that's what she needed now more than anything. Hours later, she found a small stream that somehow looked familiar and jumped into it, not even bothering to rid of potential bacteria first; she was so parched she didn't think twice about guzzling down handfuls of it.

That night, she wished she had boiled it.

Her face burned while her body shook with chills. Then came the nausea, rolling her stomach around like a piece of driftwood on a wave. She couldn't remember a time she had ever felt this ill, consciousness slipping away from her more and more frequently. By the following night, she was surprised to still be alive.

On the fifth afternoon following Frank's death, her mindless wandering in delirium found her a friendly face.

"Ella?" A familiar deep voice asked her across a meadow. She knew this meadow. It was the small clearing she had once found dandelions with Frank as a child.

"Eli?" She returned with a cracked voice, squinting with her hand over her head to shield the sun. She felt her cracked lips with her tongue, her throat just as dry. As he rushed over to her, she collapsed weakly into his arms.

"What happened to you? Where's Frank?" he questioned rapidly. She feebly shook her head. Even though her eyes were shut, she could imagine him trying to search her face for more answers. "Ella, what happened?" he whispered. Then he lowered them both to the ground, cradling her like a child.

"Water... bad," she managed to explain.

"The bottle," he said quietly. What was he talking about? Before she needed to ask, she felt him pull something out of his pocket. Opening her eyes just a crack, she saw it was a small container.

The item she had seen Frank hand him while they were all leaving.

"Here," he said quickly, "take a few." Aiella pointed at her throat, hopeful the gesture would translate to Eli. Of course it did. "Water! Yes," he replied. "Here." Reaching behind him, he grabbed a bottle, handing it to her as she opened her mouth delicately for him to place the medicine in. A lot of good the crystal had been against this. Part of her wondered if it knew not all of her wanted to heal.

After drinking the rest of the bottle of water, Aiella looked apologetically at Eli. "It's fine," he said with a chuckle. There was something else etched into his eyes and voice, though. Sadness? Concern? As the water began to hydrate her, she slowly perked up, confident that the medicine would save her. Seeing Eli care so much about her wellbeing gave her the strength needed to force herself on. She needed to do all of this for him. To find answers about herself. About Haydn. She had to do it for him. For the others. For every soul on Earth.

"When you're ready, I know everyone will be happy to see you," Eli told her tenderly, a sad smile on his face.

"You're all okay?" She asked, holding her breath. He gave a nod, and she released it. "Thank the heavens," she sighed.

"You're going to be okay, too," he replied, gently grabbing her chin.

"I know," she said quietly. Looking into his eyes, tears started forming again, the pit in her chest growing bigger and bigger. "I didn't mean to come back this way, though," she whimpered. "I must have gotten lost, and my instincts led me back, but... I have to leave again," she sniffled. "You're all in danger around me. Frank died because of me. Haydn wanted to get to me." She buried her face in his shoulder, gripping his back for dear life. "You mean too much to me, Eli," she cried. "You all do."

"You don't have to do everything alone," he said, almost as though it were a question.

"I know," she whispered. And she did. "But I can't do this with you either. You're too important for me to lose." She felt him nodding his head up and down, his throat cracking in a desperate sound that broke her heart even further.

"Where will you go?" he finally asked her, pulling back slightly to see her face. A single tear had streaked across each side of his face.

"I don't know," she responded honestly. It terrified her. The whole universe terrified her right now. She recalled what Frank had told her about not being the first to feel the weight of the world was on her shoulders, and that, with any luck, she wouldn't be the last. Somehow, she would hold on to that. Somehow, she would live up to it. As the sun started to fall behind the tops of the trees, she fell asleep briefly in Eli's arms, knowing fully well that it might be the last time she was ever close to someone she loved.

Just as she was about to say goodbye for the last time, a booming voice spoke loud and clearly through the forest. Jolted, she swung her head up, immediately regretting the quick movement. Blinking to try to regain her spinning vision, she gasped as she noticed there was more than one person standing in front of her.

"Aiella?" The same voice spoke again, looking around at the others before stepping closer to her and Eli. "Are you okay?"

"Who are you?" Aiella stood up defensively, looking around her for something to use as a weapon or shield. Eli was scurrying to do the same.

"Shh. There is no need to be scared." The woman closed in on her, gently touching her shoulder. Aiella was too weak and dizzy to object. The medicine was beginning to work, fortunately, but it couldn't work that fast. "You are suffering from the aftermath of using your abilities," the woman frowned, her gaze setting in on the stone ebbing around her neck. It had been purple for the past couple of hours.

"What are you talking about?" Aiella squinted. "How do you know my name? Who are you?" Her lips trembled, extreme thirst still prevalent, though her stance remained defiant.

"I am Eloquine, Vice Chairman of the Elemental Council," the woman said, reaching a hand out. *The Elemental Council.* That was in the letter from Zale! She looked the people in front of her up and down, the gown of Eloquine glistening with a strange, magical glow much like the crystal she had on her chest. "These are my colleagues Aisling, Burgin, and Cillian," she explained, gesturing to the other three accompanying her. "We are from Satera, and we have come to take you home."

Aiella's head was spinning. Satera? How far had they traveled? Her vision blurring, she lay down, breathing deeply as she stared at the tree line ahead of her. The earth gave her energy; this much she had learned recently. With her fingers digging into the cool dirt, she debated what she should do. The only way to ever find answers was to go with them, but...

"How do we know this isn't a trap?" Eli asked boldly, speaking her mind for her.

She sat up, burying her face in her hands. Images of Frank and the others flashed through her mind, her heart aching. She wished she could stay with them, the depth of how lonely and lost she was without them drowning her like a turbulent wave on an unsuspecting shore. She could feel the ground below her begin to tremble again. Her mind and body weakened, though, it quickly stopped.

She needed these people before her to be who they said they were. She needed someone to know who she was. Someone who could help give her a chance at saving her family. She affected the world around her; the pain she felt when nature was afflicted was too obvious to ignore. The Elemental Council might be the only souls in the universe who could answer her questions and save the ones she loved. Before she could talk, Eloquine spoke again, her hand still reached out awkwardly as she looked at the others.

"I know this is a lot to take in," she said tenderly. "And we are all so sorry for your loss."

Aiella jumped to her feet, regretting it as white spots formed. "How do you know that?" She demanded, sitting back down as fast as she had stood.

"Are you all right?" Eli asked, rushing over to her. He glared at the Council before them. "She needs to rest."

"We have seen most of the trials you have conquered so far, Aiella," Eloquine whispered, ignoring Eli's remark.

"But how?" Aiella questioned. "I'm okay," she added softly to Eli.

"Because you're one of us," Eloquine answered simply.

"If you've been watching her this entire time, why didn't you step in to help us?" Eli queried. Aiella nodded vigorously in agreement.

"Why didn't you save my grandmother? Or Frank?" Angry water poured from her face, her hands unexpectedly balled into fists. "You could have saved them!" She shouted. "Why should I trust you to help me now?" Eli reached his arm out to hers, finding her hand and giving it a squeeze. She took a deep breath, shutting her eyes.

"Your grandmother was on a mission," Eloquine spoke after a pause. "A mission set forth long ago. That crystal you have around your neck," she said with a gesture of her hand, "was meant to get into your hands when you turned 18. Anytime before then and you might have been found by Haydn before your powers could protect you. Your grandmother waited until it was the right time to retrieve it."

"Why would a crystal lead Haydn to me prematurely?" She queried. "Why did I need to be 18?"

"Until someone like you has reached 18, their powers are quite flexible. While training usually begins at a younger age, we couldn't risk Haydn being the first one to show you what power looked like when you had such an impressionable mind. You have always meant to bring hope, not darkness."

"And what's that have to do with this strange crystal?" She persisted, clutching her hand around it. Eloquine raised an eyebrow and smiled.

"You haven't figured out that it's connected to you? It was made as a means to help you control and harness abilities like yours. Athena, your grandmother, actually helped to create it. She was always going to be the one who undertook your training after she retrieved the stone. You weren't going to come along to Satera until you were more prepared. Until you had had time for all of this to sink in. But I'm afraid things have changed." She frowned, the others behind her bowing their heads. "Athena was a good woman. Loved by many. We are so sorry, Ella. And...?" She looked at Eli expectantly.

"Eli," he grunted.

"Eli," Eloquine repeated. "We are sorry for both of your losses." He gave a curt nod before turning his eyes to the dirt.

Aiella bit her tongue until it bled. Everything she thought she knew, everything that Frank thought he knew, being thrown out forever.

"It will be easier to explain in detail once we are back to Satera," Eloquine urged. "Please. We need to go now. It won't be safe here for long."

"How am I supposed to --"

"Use this transportation pad," she told her, handing her a disk no larger than her hand. Aiella stared back at her.

"This is how I get to Satera?" she laughed in disbelief. She looked at Eli, who raised an eyebrow with a half-laugh.

"This is a whole new level of weird," he shrugged. Eloquine wore a solemn look on her face that told Aiella it was indeed. Upon grabbing it, a low whirring filled her. The others were pulling their own pads out, each a slightly different hue, and swiping them before placing them on the ground.

"Yours is already activated," Eloquine spoke loudly. "It can be... chaotic... for first-time users." Whatever that meant, her life was always a mess.

Heaving a deep breath, Aiella set her pad carefully on the earth in front of her. *Please let this be the right move,* she prayed. She looked at Eli, who had already begun to step away.

"You've made your choice, then?"

"You know I don't have a choice," Aiella pleaded. All she wanted was to get answers about her past that might help save her family's future. Alexis and Luke and Eli and the others. They were all she had left. Her heart sank, hoping Zale remained alive, too. The pearly reflection of the pad was reminiscent of the stones she used to collect from the riverbank when she was younger. It was mesmerizing. She swallowed back tears, images of Frank in her early years flooding to her like a swarm of bees.

"I know," he said. But at that moment, Aiella wasn't so sure.

"We step on three," Eloquine instructed.

"Hear, hear," the other three confirmed.

"Ella?" she asked.

"Hear, hear," she said quietly, her stomach flip flopping in anticipation of what was about to happen.

"One." Aiella looked up at the others, positioned and looking as though they were about to run. She squatted in a similar stance.

"Two." She inhaled and held her breath, wrapping a hand around the necklace and patting her shirt to ensure she still had Zale's letter. It was there, though possibly charred. Eli's lips met her cheek, ever-so-briefly, before disappearing, his body rushing quickly away as Aiella tried to get one last look at him.

"Three." Stepping in unison, Aiella saw the others disappear into a flash of light, and then she was flying, leaving everything she ever loved and knew below her.

Chapter 25

"Ella!"

Eli's shout up to Aiella was the last sound she heard on Earth. A scream immediately tried to escape Aiella's lips in return, but was repressed by the sheer force surrounding her, threatening to rip her apart limb by limb. Her eyes swiftly squeezed tightly shut, trying to find a reason strong enough to open them again. Her thoughts swirled in a never ending vortex, flashes of Frank and her grandmother and Haydn and Zale all whirling together in chaos. When she was sure she had been in the air for too long, unsure whether she was still going up or was now falling down, she dared to take a peek.

The light around her was blinding, a sheen golden white enclosing her in a tunnel that shot perfectly up and down. Her body was paralyzed in its rigid position, although her eyes could move around enough to make out what was beyond the sheer curtain she was speeding through. Squinting, she saw Eloquine and the others encased in different colored beams, rocketing through the sky beside her. It was as if they were all creating separate beams of a rainbow. They looked so peaceful, the blue, yellow, and green tones surely a beautiful light show for those down below. She hoped that Eli would take the tribe far away from here, and that the others would forgive her when he told them her choice. She hoped as he watched this that Eli understood too. This was about something bigger. It had always been about something bigger. It just had taken her too long to figure it out. As a result... Well, the loss was too great to bear. If she could travel back in time, she would. Who knew how long Frank had instructed the tribe to stay in the backup tunnels, but she prayed it wasn't long. Who knew if Haydn was really dead. If he managed to survive, he would stop at nothing to destroy them.

Suddenly, Aiella felt the force around her easing, gasping as they broke through the atmosphere and into the dark reign of space. How was she able to gasp? She had a little more freedom to move now and made small motions with her head to look around. It felt as though she should be falling, and maybe she was? She wished she had something to hold on to, although the beam she was enclosed inside seemed it was cradling her well enough. Breathtaking clusters of constellations and gasses formed clouds far off in the distance, the earth a formidable marble of all of her favorite hues, becoming more visible in its entirety by the second as she flew further and further away. How was she breathing?

The darkness was astounding. She always dreamed of space, always imagined what it would be like to soar through the sky, hurtling towards the great unknown, but never in a million years did she think she would be here. The craziest part was that this wasn't the first time. Earth was never her true home, as much as it felt like it. Had this been the mode of transportation for her when she arrived as a toddler? If so, she was a brave little baby. The thought gave her chills. Or maybe it was the extremely freezing temperature from the lack of particles outside of her lit-up safe space. Never had she felt so grateful Frank had taught her about the universe as much as he could. Had he known even more than he let on? Or at least suspect it? He had to have.

The craters up ahead were nothing short of incredible as they tumbled towards the moon. Frank had always shown her space and the moon from all of his old textbooks, always fascinated in science's latest discoveries, but this was a million times more amazing than she could ever have fathomed! For a moment, she forgot she was suspended in nothingness in ways that the modern science she knew never could have explained. It was... freeing.

The surface of the moon was much larger and brighter than expected, and though the wispy beam she was enclosed in seemed to lessen the radiation reaching Aiella's eyes, she still felt inclined to close them. Scared they might go plummeting onto the surface, she dared open her eyes partially, if only for a few seconds. The moon was below her now, the beam's path ahead seeming to curve. Squealing, she felt more force being pressed on her again as she thought she saw another moon, a fraction the size of Earth's, coming into view.

A satellite of some sort?

Since chemistry and light were topics she was so interested in, Frank had told her long ago of the theory of sub moons existing in the solar systems, or around exoplanets, but still no evidence had been found of them before the outbreak. And yet... She was certain as she zipped through space that she was now circling the far side of the moon, and there was definitely another, smaller planet of some type straight ahead. Not a man-made satellite, or another moon, but a tiny planet. Reds and greens and chunks of blue were visible on the surface, like all the geographic anomalies of Earth had been captured and shrunk down to a large model. Hidden behind the moon. She clasped her eyes shut again, feeling a bit queasy. They had to be traveling faster than a human body should be able to handle. There was no way to deduce the time out here, but it felt like they had only been traveling a few minutes.

Impossible.

Yet here she was.

A whirring feeling filled her again, this time not as intense as before. They must almost be arriving. That small planet before her must be Satera. Excitement trembled through her skin and bones, her body adjusting to the gradual changes in velocity as they neared the surface.

As quickly as she had been lifted off the earthen soil, she found herself standing on what she knew in her gut was Sateran ground.

"You can open your eyes now," she heard Cillian say with a laugh. She slowly peeled them open, Eloquine, Aisling, and Burgin all in front of her, though Cillian's fingers were over her face.

"Let her looksee, then!" Burgin demanded playfully. Drawing his hands away dramatically, Cillian and the others watched her as Satera stared back at Aiella in all its glory.

"It's beautiful," she whispered. Aisling smiled, and she could hear Cillian chuckle again. Before her in the valley was an expanse of beautiful stone buildings so smooth, they looked like glass. The moon loomed over the planet, a large, but comforting object in the skyline. Being this close to it felt strange, but simultaneously as normal as seeing a formidable mountain standing tall. It looked like it was daytime here, though the horizon ahead was filled with fluffy purple and yellow clouds that made it seem otherwise. Though it was hard to make out details, beyond the gorgeous architectural basin was a forest and lake of some sort.

"There is more behind you," Eloquine informed her softly, a grin on what Aiella had grown to think was an always serious face.

Spinning around slowly, Aiella looked up in awe. They were standing in front of another stone building, but this one was literally filled with glass. Windows went from ceiling to rooftop in some spots, and the building had to be at least ten stories tall. In other spots, colorful glass and ceramics of varying shapes formed pieces of art in the shape of a wave, leaf, flame, and one other object that she couldn't place. A spiral of sorts. It reminded her of stained glass she had read about, but this was three dimensional and more opaque. Giant columns were on either side of the building, engraved in a language she couldn't understand, with a matching rounded triangle insignia stamped onto the bottom of each.

They, and the stunning building, were up on a huge platform, with each side of the building leading to steps that looked to lead down to more of the beautiful smaller buildings she had originally laid her eyes on. However, while those first ones in the valley were short and square, these were taller and more circular, the outsides all mismatching faint shades of blues, greens, tans, and reds. *Amazing*. Each building looked to have a balcony, and off in the distance, Aiella was certain she heard children giggling. *Children!* Life was abound. The sound filled her with a sense of ease and happiness that was unparalleled. She was *home*.

"Incredible," she said breathlessly, still spinning in circles to take in everything around her.

"Welcome to the Elemental Headquarters of the Sateran Council," Eloquine proudly stated.

Chapter 26

"This is where you work?" Aiella gasped. The clothing Eloquine was wearing explained a lot. It was all especially fitting now. This place was unbelievable.

"Where we all work," she replied. "I just happen to have a bigger office."

"I can't believe it..." Aiella muttered in wonder. Would she get the opportunity to work here? She couldn't imagine having a real job, let alone one in such a majestic location. She pinched herself. Surely this had to be a dream!

"Still?" Cillian sighed. "You would think after the trip here and all you have been through that you might trust it was real."

Aiella nervously laughed, dropping her hand. The pinch hurt. "No, no. I just... It's hard. My whole life has been spent in an underground cave, and now... this. It is incredible. I am so lucky. I just wish my other family were here to see it." She hung her head sadly, thinking of Eli and the others. Imagine the look on Alexis' face if she could be here! She and Luke could have the sweetest life in one of those towers—high in the sky instead of beneath the dirt.

"We are your family now, too," Eloquine placed a hand on her shoulder. "Welcome home, Aiella." She gave a stern look to the other three, and they started to leave. "Thank you for your assistance." With a nod, they headed off. She turned her attention back to Aiella. "Was not nearly as exciting of a trip as I am sure they wanted. I'm happy we didn't have any trouble, though."

"Will be around, though, Aiella!" She heard one of them yell back. A smirk forced itself across her lips, helping her to relax.

"What do you mean, troubles?" She couldn't help but ask.

"Come," Eloquine stuck her arm out, avoiding the question. She ushered Aiella towards the large, beautiful building before them. "We have much to discuss."

The interior of the building was just as impressive as the outside. If she thought Haydn knew how to make an enchanting fortress, this place was the dream version. He was from this planet and wanted to leave? Why would anyone ever? Though it felt eerie in its unfamiliarity, the lobby entrance alone was stunning enough to make Aiella want to stay here forever. Her trepidation in the days before was all melting far away from her, the present moment clearly what had been meant to be all along.

All the many windows, which did have some stained glass scattered throughout after all, let the most angelic arrays of light into everyone. The floors were reflective, small rainbows seeming to exist indoors from the tiny rays bouncing off. Aiella was reminded again why she liked spectroscopy. Frank would be so proud of her being a "nerd," she thought she remembered him referring to it as. Just like him. The hole in her heart grew, threatening to have another emotional outburst again, but it faded as quickly as it had come, the setting before her too grand to ignore. Gigantic spiral staircases were on either side of the large room, with a strange door in between, a door frequently opening and shutting as people went in and out.

"Our own version of an elevator," Eloquine told her.

"Elevator?" Aiella asked.

"Ah. Right. Underground. You must forgive me; I forget you aren't accustomed to all of this yet. You will be in due time, I assure you! An elevator is a simple contraption that humans created to lift objects up and down. Our version is much faster, and therefore more efficient."

"Are we going to go on it?" She swallowed.

"Yes. My office is near the top floor. You aren't scared, are you?" She asked, a hand meeting her chin in surprise. "Dear Aiella, you already have used a transportation pad, and this is not nearly as sophisticated. We will just be going to the top of the building, not to another planet. After all you have been through, this will be easy." She was being serious, but Aiella could sense the well-intended humor beneath the words.

"I suppose you're right," Aiella replied slowly. She began to shrug, then suddenly stopped. "Shoot! My transportation pad. I never picked it up after we landed!"

"Oh, that's long gone," Eloquine told her, waving her hand around mindlessly. "The amount of energy required to travel like that is tremendous. They are only meant for single use."

As they arrived in front of the two opening doors, Eloquine placed her hand on a clear glass on the wall. "My handprint, so the correct pulley comes," she explained before Aiella could ask. *How sophisticated.* When the contraption arrived, Aiella stepped inside, admiring the craftsmanship. After giving her a moment, Eloquine pushed a series of buttons to the side of her. "Here we go," she smiled. "You may want to hold on." She gestured to a handle on the side of the cube they were in, and Aiella jumped to it, clinging on tightly. Hardly a full second later, they were tumbling upward, Aiella's ringlets dancing around her face briefly, and Eloquine's dark features stood out as her smooth black hair straightened even more. The pulley, as she had called it, came to an abrupt stop before Aiella could even catch her breath.

When the doors opened, Eloquine stepped out casually, clearly used to the ride they had just been on. "Come," she beckoned. "Those doors won't stay open long."

Shaking, Aiella hurried out of the pulley just as it slammed shut behind her. Inhaling as deeply as her lungs would allow, she noticed the vice chairwoman had already taken a seat on a large cushioned seat near the window. Jogging nonchalantly to join her, the view was spectacular. All the pearly buildings she had seen outside looked smaller, more uniform, and more unbelievably stunning from up here. The clouds were still a yellowy purple color, but she could see far beyond the small city to the edge of the horizon from up here. There was a lake, as she had thought, but also it seemed many hills, large expanses of glistening gold, and more clusters of trees than she originally imagined. If not for the architecture made of a stone Aiella had never heard of, it looked an awful lot like Earth. Just as it had from space. Well, the moon here was much larger, of course. Still the same moon, though. That thought gave her comfort.

"Is it daytime here?" Aiella asked, still standing in front of the expanse of glass and views.

"Yes, though our days look quite a bit different here than yours did on Earth."

"Are they longer?" She questioned. "Or shorter? Or?"

"Much longer," Eloquine said pleasantly. "Come sit." She pointed out the chair next to her, crossing her legs and leaning forward. "Right now is towards the beginning of our day, as you would call it. It is close to a couple of weeks of some form of daylight, followed by a couple of weeks of varying shades of dark. The phase of lightness is called Lux, while the phase of dark that follows is called Tene. We have a lot of technology that helps us regulate on normal days, though, following Earth's hours since that is the planet we currently serve."

"Currently serve?" Aiella asked. Finally, she would ask the questions that mattered.

"Satera is one of many planets we have created and called home over the past several billions of years. You really should sit." She gestured again to the chair beside her. Aiella obliged, the cushion immensely softer than any she had sat on before. A happy sigh fell from her breath as Eloquine continued. "We - the Elementals - have journeyed through much of the universe, helping maintain and restore balance to hundreds upon thousands of solar systems, planets, and forms of life. Those born on the sub planet they are raised are called just that. For example, we are all Saterans, from this beautiful home of Satera. However, we are all still Elementals. It is our ancestry, and we exist to protect.

"I am sure you noticed the color of the sky when you arrived, being as tuned in to science and chemistry as you are." Aiella gave her a questioning look before remembering they said they had been keeping tabs on her. "We have different elements here than you might find on Earth; ones that have been gathered over the many millennia of travelling. Though well over a hundred elements had been discovered by Earthen scientists before the outbreak halted much research, many, *many* more exist. Many are simply not within their reach. Science and technology have not evolved thoroughly enough for those on Earth yet to travel and understand space and time as well as we have come to.

"Out past the capital limits," she pointed beyond the smooth, pale buildings. Aiella realized for the first time a quick moving train of sorts on a raised rail going out towards the horizon. "Are regions for each of the four elements we harness and protect on Earth. There is the Aer region, in charge of protecting air, filled with flowing prairies and much open space. Ignis, the fire region, is home to an active volcano and a river of lava. You can probably make out the large lake in Acqua - the water region. And finally, there is the sector of Terra, or the earth element. All of these - Aer,

Acqua, Ignis, and Terra - make up the essence of Earth, and they are the elements which we are sworn to protect."

"So, are you guys like gods...?" Aiella pondered. It occurred to her she should start referring to Saterans as "us," but it felt too soon.

"In a way, yes," Eloquine responded. "But in many other ways, no. More so, we are peacemakers for the planet. While we love most of all living creatures, humans included, with this assignment we are not here solely for that. We are not to harm them, but our primary focus is Earth herself. Not the creatures that inhabit Her."

"Guardians of the Earth and Her elements..." Aiella thought out loud.

"Precisely."

"What does everyone do for work here? And if not all elements are the same here on Satera, how do the plants in each of those regions grow? It is so similar to Earth."

Eloquine smiled at her cleverness. "It is good to have such an earnest Guardian."

"Yeah, I've been told I ask a lot of questions," Aiella started. But then she froze. "Wait. Guardian?" Her heart skipped a beat as she sat forward. A guardian? Her? What was she talking about?

"Each element has a protector. Sometimes more than one, though that is quite rare. These elementals possess magical abilities that allow them to best harness and protect the element they are attached to. The element becomes a part of them. These protectors are called Elemental Guardians," Eloquine explained slowly.

"What does that have to do with me?" Aiella asked tentatively. She held her breath, waiting for the answer.

"You are an Elemental Guardian, Aiella. The Guardian of Terra."

If Aiella had had food in her mouth, she would have spat it out in shock. "You must have me mistaken," she shook her head fervently.

"Nope," Eloquine replied, "and I know that you believe it." Aiella still shook her head quickly, wanting to mutter "no," but finding no words could come out. Eloquine merely kept giving slow nods. Eventually, Aiella found her croaking voice again.

"My powers, as you called them…" she said quietly. "They're meant to protect Earth."

Eloquine nodded patiently. "The surge of energy that released itself in the form of an earthquake has occurred since you are now of age and have had no formal training. When you become of age as an Elemental, you are assigned your duty usually. Guardians are a bit different, though, beginning training as soon as they learn their duties so that they are as ready as possible when their elements bond permanently with them at the start of their nineteenth year. You were always going to be different since you were brought to Earth indefinitely, not to return until Athena had trained you. Nevertheless, it's a hard obstacle to overcome. The signs that someone will be a Guardian are sometimes prophesied before they are born, and other times they are revealed when one Guardian passes on. In the latter situation, the soul of the power attaches to the nearest child or adolescent. You were the former. When you turned 18, you bonded permanently with your element, causing a little havoc whenever your emotions got the best of you. Fortunately, you had that crystal to assist you in harnessing some of the abilities. It's a very powerful relic."

"Training would fix that? It would help me control myself more?"

"Indeed. And we will get to that. We already have it arranged for you to begin training shortly. You have a lot of catching up to do."

"Are the other Guardians my age as well? What does everyone else do that isn't a Guardian?" Aiella stood up, beginning to pace.

"Aenon isn't much older than you. He is the Elemental Guardian of Acqua. Other Elementals, such as myself, busy themselves in public service roles. Both to keep Satera running, and to keep tabs on Earth so that the Guardians can protect the elements as easily as possible."

"If there are four elements, shouldn't there be four Elemental Guardians?" Aiella questioned.

"Yes..." Eloquine spoke carefully. "Sometimes there are more, too, though that is very rare and has only ever happened a couple of times since the start of the universe." Aiella stared at her. Four or more?

"Are there three others then?" She pushed.

"I'm afraid not. Currently, there are only three Elemental Guardians in total. One holds more than one of the elements. Something unheard of before now." She watched Aiella carefully, making her think she should know more than she did.

"Who is the other?" Aiella questioned slowly.

"You haven't guessed it by now?" Eloquine raised an eyebrow.

Aiella stared out at the vast expanse before her, still in awe of the view. She was sure her eyes were deceiving her, but far beyond the glisten of water, she thought she could make out the volcano Eloquine spoke of a moment ago. "Haydn," she whispered. When Eloquine was silent, she twirled around to face her. "He's a Guardian? And on Earth?"

"I am afraid so," she told her curtly.

"He's destroying it!" She yelled. "How is this allowed? Why would he do it?" She demanded with a ferocity she didn't know she had in her.

"He believes that he is fighting a good cause. That humans have tarnished the Earth that we are supposed to protect." So that was, in fact, what Zale meant. "And well, as for how he did it... He corrupted so many people's minds here that the Council ended up disbanded. Until recently."

"How long was the disbandment?" Aiella asked.

"About twenty years." Aiella ran her hands through her frizzy curls, trying to comprehend all this new information.

"Oh no," she gasped. "He isn't the one with two elements, is he? It's Aenon?"

"Well, actually... We have reason to believe it is you." Aiella just gaped at her.

"You've got to be kidding me. I don't even know how to not cause earthquakes, and now you are saying I harness another power?"

"Ability to wield an element," she corrected. "But yes. We have reason to believe that you are also the Elemental Guardian of Aer."

"Why would you think that?" Aiella asked. "I mean, Terra I could see. The earth was always working in my favor. But air? What have I done that would hint at that ability?"

"It's actually the other way around, frankly. You were told to be the Guardian of Aer but have shown strong indications of wielding earth."

Aiella did not know what to say as a response, so figured she might as well keep pressing for answers.

"What happened to my parents?" She questioned, unsure if she wanted to know the answer. "Was one of them a Guardian?"

"Actually, they were both Guardians - another rare occurrence. Perhaps that is why you are so special. Not long after you were born, a prophecy spoke of a Guardian who would be able to rid the world of Haydn's corruption that was well underway, the disease then starting its spread on innocent humans. That is where you get the prefix of your name - "Ai," meaning hope. Not all believe in that sort of thing, but your parents loved you more than anything and didn't want to risk being wrong. Knowing you would be protected from his illness being an Elemental, you were sent to Earth with your grandmother. You were to go into hiding, away from harm until you were older. We sent spies down eventually. It was easy enough with our ranks leaving to join him in secret, here and then. The guard you met, Zale, was one of them. Your grandmother was told to retrieve that crystal just before you turned 18," she pointed to the object around Aiella's neck. "An object that our spy was carefully given just a few weeks ago. One that would hopefully aid in your safe return home after training. I'm glad that even with your grandmother gone, you and Zale were able to complete that critical part of the task. It was created to help you, and in turn aid in defeating the darkness that Haydn has caused."

"And he killed my parents," she mumbled. Though the question remained *how*, if Elementals were immune to the outbreak?

"Unfortunately, yes. Your father died in a battle not long after you were brought down to Earth with your grandmother, and your mother died a few years later after heading to Earth to try to find you. Haydn followed, of course. You mustn't blame yourself." How could she not? The room began to spin as Eloquine droned on. "He had done much of his dirty work from afar before then, you see. When your mother left, it confirmed you must be on Earth. He could not risk your defeating him when he was making such progress on his plans. That's when ceremotosis found the Pacific Northwest. He had only been to the Eastern sector to hit the most populated areas with the disease before then. Figured he could wipe out a large group at once and people would make wiser choices when they had to rebuild. It was all rather isolated until he realized it was contagious. He never meant it to be able to spread to others through human contact. I guess it worked in his favor," she added thoughtfully.

"He's adept in much of Earthen science..." Aiella whispered. He must have started studying it even more after his creation started turning into a contagious virus. He hadn't planned on that all along? Aiella didn't know whether she should feel relieved or more afraid.

"He is," Eloquine confirmed. "Setting up in Volcry, experimenting using a blend of science from our world and Earth has been his priority. Aside from hunting down you." Aiella nodded, thinking of the tanks of strange liquids and plasmas meant to destroy her. What did he know that they didn't yet?

"The disease... You think he has a grasp on it by now?" Aiella asked.

"Ceremotosis?"

"Yes."

"I would imagine so. It's been a while, and I know he still studies it. Hasn't used it in quite some time, though."

"That's not true," Aiella said softly. "He used it to kill him... Frank. Except it accelerated extremely rapidly. He was gone within a day." She choked back sobs as the words came from her mouth. The Pacific Northwest region had only ever been hit with the strange contagion because of her. Because he had been searching for her. The Eastern sector was to prove his point, but... The rest. That was because he wanted her dead and was trying to fish her out. The weight of multiple worlds and millions of lives settled back onto her shoulders, but she was becoming too numb to cry.

"Did my mom ever find me? Do I just not remember?" Her voice broke, but she forced it to regrow immediately.

"Your mother brought her second baby along and sacrificed her life before finding you. I'm sorry," Eloquine said with a frown.

"This must all be a lot for you. Perhaps you should get some rest. I can show you your new home, or your old--"

"Wait, I had a sibling?" Aiella cut her off.

"Yes... A sister."

"Sister?"

"Your mother sacrificed her life for her. She's still..." She spoke slowly before clearing her throat and continuing. "Your sister... She's alive. You've been with her all this time. I figured you might have known?" Aiella gasped, her eyes widening as she thought of the one girl in the world she loved more than anything.

Chapter 27

Aiella could not believe that she had not seen it before. She had always considered both Alexis and Luke to be like siblings to her, but the overwhelming sense of protection she felt inclined to give Alexis should have had her knowing there was something more. Plus, she was Sateran just like her. How did she not piece everything together sooner?

"Argh!" she screamed over the faint sound of music. The past hour was a blur, only those same repetitive thoughts falling through her mind as she walked through the motions of Eloquine introducing her to her new housing arrangement. One that included music played from inside the walls. She found it both relaxing and aggravating. She wasn't used to having something like it invade her thoughts. Not having the energy to figure out how to turn it off, she decided a bath would be a good idea - as Eloquine had suggested before she left.

Entering the washroom, she had to catch her breath when she saw herself for the first time in something other than water's reflection. She walked on tiptoe to the smooth piece of glass before her, touching it where her face was. Compared to what Eloquine appeared as, she was a disaster. Her hair was in complete disarray, hanging down her back and around her shoulders in as inelegant of a way as possible, the smallest of twigs sticking out here and there. Her dark lips were cracked and looked purple-tinged, an uneasy contrast against her tan skin. Her face was still bloodied and bruised, her cheekbones gaunt from the events of the past few days. The only thing extraordinary about her right now was her vibrant eyes, each one shining a different color. Were they that way because she could wield two different elements? A brilliant blue for aer, a sparkling golden hue to represent terra? Everyone's eye colors here were piercing and vibrant, making it hard to look away. But still, she hadn't seen someone with two different colors yet. She couldn't help but wonder if it did have to do with being an Elemental Guardian. Though Haydn's both seemed the same electrifying red color... But fire was his element. What had her parents looked like? What about the Guardian of Acqua - Aenon, was it?

On their long walk over to her new home, Eloquine had explained that all living beings could communicate in some way. Even some nonliving could, but not nearly as efficiently. She told her that protecting an element and wielding abilities reflecting it could be broken down as simply being able to communicate in that language with them. Which explained the sensation she became afflicted with when trees were cut wrong. Or burned. She was one with them, and they spoke to her. They had her back, and she had theirs. That's how it worked in theory, at least. Aiella sighed. It was like she was starting school as a young child, except she was supposed to be a master by now. And she had never been formally educated before.

Luckily, she was able to figure out how to start the bath just fine. The water came out of a metal spout, not unlike the one that brought them the water into the tunnels from the waterfall. Placing a foot in the hot water was unlike the community pool in so many ways. The water there had sat for so long it was tinted green, with a slimy texture coating you when you got out. You had to go in with undergarments on since it was public, and it wasn't like they had an abundance of hygienic products to cleanse them. Frank had poured some chemicals in it at the beginning that quickly faded, and otherwise it had salt tablets thrown in every once in a while. Where Frank kept them stored, she had no idea. Kind of disgusting to look back on, really. This new world was so much more elegant than the one she had just left, and it was filled with what many had once considered basic necessities.

Having poured way too much soap inside, the bubbles were frothy and fragrant, inviting her in with such a giddy aura she couldn't help but unwind as she slipped under them, her filthy clothes landing on the floor. So this was what a bath was supposed to be like. She let herself soak in the warm jets, her skin wrinkling at her fingertips and toes - should she be worried about that? After her mind became clearer, the fizz of the soap long gone, and the water now a murky gray color, Aiella stepped out of the porcelain tub a new version of herself.

The mirror she had gazed in was fogged with condensation, so she waited. As it became clear, the reflection revealed a large cabinet behind her. Her hands trailed along the magnificent craftsmanship, appreciating that it was made of some kind of light rock instead of oak. Releasing the latch, the door opened and a beautiful silky gown fell out. Eloquine must have set them here before coming for her.

She fumbled through the bottom drawer below the drawer, desperate to find underwear so she didn't have to put her dirty clothes back on. Then again, she could wash them thoroughly in that tub with all the soap she now had. *Bingo.*

To her delight, the bottom drawer was filled with not only several pieces of undergarments, but plain shirts and pants as well. As gorgeous as the dress was, there was no way she could train in it. It occurred to her for the first time there may be events or reasons she would need the gown, though. She was practically royalty now, after all. The thought sent shivers down her spine, a whole new kind of nervousness setting in. She wasn't just responsible for the tribe anymore, but an entire element. *Two of them.* She was meant to protect an entire planet.

After she was dressed comfortably, she sat on the floor, staring at the bathroom of her new home. Was this real? Everything was elegant, and clean, and... non-threatening. There weren't bobcats waiting for her outside her room, or a mysterious illness lurking in the city. All mystery of the illness she had grown up around had recently vanished, anyway. She inhaled a deep breath, one full of damp but fresh-smelling air, and exhaled out more than she had realized she was holding onto. That's when she saw the small piece of paper folded neatly at the bottom of the open shelf her new gown was hanging over.

Aiella gasped as she opened the paper to reveal a small picture. A young woman stared back at her, with a huge grin on her face. Below her hip, clinging to her hand and smiling up at her, was a tiny girl with short, curly hair. Aiella felt her hand instinctively reach for her locks now, all these years later.

"Mom," she whispered, rubbing her thumb gently over the image. She brought it to her chest, tears streaming down her face. She reached out, grabbing the edge of the beautiful dress again, its soft fibers caressing her as it gave off an effervescent glow reflecting the surrounding lights.

It had been her mother's.

Chapter 28

A knock at the door woke Aiella from her whirlwind thoughts.

"Come in!" she yelled.

Eloquine walked in, with a tall man by her side. Something about him looked familiar, but she could not place why.

"I hope you managed to sleep all right," Eloquine told her tenderly, a concerned smile on her face.

"Hardly," Aiella said plainly, her gaze returning to the large window of her apartment. She had learned that the buildings on either side of the Elemental Headquarters were for the Elemental Guardians and their families. Since her parents had both been Guardians in the past, she now had plenty of space for just herself. She preferred the new apartment they offered her to the home she once shared with her biological family. She recalled that, a few weeks back, she was caught up in imagining what her home as an infant was like. And now, here she was, able to go to it. Live in it, even. She always imagined home was on Earth, though. That it had a fence around the backyard, with flowers and trees lining the property... Maybe there was a pond. She had yet to decide if this was an upgrade to her imagination or not.

Too much new information had surfaced, and she knew that living within the exact same walls she had as a baby would only lead to more emotional turmoil. Something she knew she could not afford before having some form of training completed. The gown last night had proven that. As soon as she realized the connection to her mother, it was as though an isolated windstorm had swept through her apartment. She spent most of the evening just cleaning up and was choosing to keep that to herself. She had to learn how to handle both elements she was one with and sworn to protect and restore before she could handle being in her old home with old memories lurking about.

Besides, this model had a giant balcony that wrapped around her floor, allowing plenty of breathing room to think. The views were unparalleled, too.

As Eloquine had explained in more detail later last night when she came to check in on her with dinner - something Aiella could definitely get used to - the sky looked the way it did since their atmosphere was so unique. It was not made up of the same elements that Earth's was; hence, the different shades of color. However, they were almost mirrors of the elements that those on Earth needed to thrive. Different galaxies, different creatures, different needs that spanned across millions of light years. Aiella still was unsure how they had not been discovered when humans trekked to the far side of the moon, but Eloquine had simply waved her hand, laughing. The gesture had Aiella feeling as though some people had discovered it, but either sworn to secrecy or had their minds cleared. Given the way that Haydn had manipulated her thoughts, and the fact that he had single-handedly caused the destruction from ceremotosis, Aiella honestly believed anything was possible at this point. Her heart sank, physically paining her, at the uncertainty of the safety of her younger sister and the others she loved dearly. She only hoped her training would enlighten her more and allow her to help.

"Perhaps now is a bad time," she heard the man whisper to Eloquine. She blinked, shaking her head and walking to join them.

"Apologies." Aiella extended a hand, snapping out of her downward-spiraling thoughts. "I am Aiella. It's nice to meet you."

"Lachlan," he told her, grabbing her hand, and bowing. "It is an honor."

"You don't have to do that," Aiella told him, referring to his stance.

"Such is the custom," Eloquine replied. "You'll get used to it. You are one of the highest rank in the universe now, Aiella."

She swallowed, nodding slowly as she nonchalantly tried to straighten her posture. She was sure they both saw right through her.

"Lachlan is the father of the guard who helped you escape," Eloquine continued.

"Zale?" Aiella asked incredulously.

"That's the one!" Lachlan smiled. "I see my son left quite an impression."

"I--Uh--Well. I mean. He saved me," she blurted out, feeling her cheeks flushing to the color of a cherry blossom.

"I'm just thankful he is okay, and still on the right side!" He winked.

"We know he is all right, then?" Aiella asked. Hope began to fill her chest again, before instantly diminishing. If he was okay, then that might mean that her family was not...

"We don't know anything conclusive right now," Eloquine shot a glare to Lachlan, who looked down. "We would love to believe Haydn is gone by his own fiery means." Aiella nodded slowly, her ears still burning.

"Anyway," Eloquine turned her focus entirely to Aiella, "Lachlan is an Alchimia. He possesses the ability to harness elements but is not a Guardian himself. He has devoted his life to being a trainer of other young Alchimia, as well as Guardians when another, Elder Guardian, is not present to do so themselves. I thought I would introduce you before you start training first thing in the morning. It will be the middle of Lux, a perfect time for you to begin your first lessons since the elements should be more predictable and work in your favor."

"So, do most Elementals have powers then?" Aiella pondered.

"A fair amount, but nowhere close to all. And, as you may have noticed with Haydn, Guardians have a unique ability to manipulate thoughts. It's how they best persuade the elements to work in their favor." Aiella thought about that. How Haydn had read her thoughts, how he seemed to have the citizens of Volcry brainwashed. She shuddered, realizing she had already used that ability once with Frank as well. He had heard the thoughts she projected to him. Did that make her as much of a monster as the enemy? No one should have their mind or body invaded in any way.

Aiella looked at Lachlan, a miserable scowl on his face, likely since Eloquine had scolded him moments ago. "I see you found your new clothes in the dresser," Eloquine told her, looking at her up and down. She nodded, hoping to avoid any conversation about the gown for the time being. With nothing else to say, Eloquine turned to leave, Lachlan following suit.

"Wait!" Aiella spoke out. "Could I do something tonight?"

"You are free to roam the city limits whenever you would like. You are a Guardian after all," Eloquine raised an eyebrow. "What did you have in mind?"

"I was hoping that I might be able to mourn my adoptive father," she said softly. "I know that Athena will have a service here soon, but I would love to honor him, too. The sooner, the better."

"Of course," she gave a quick nod. "I will send to have something arranged."

As they both started to leave, Aiella rapidly spoke again. "Eloquine?" She asked. "May I have a minute with you alone?" She gave an apologetic look to Lachlan before Eloquine nodded in his direction, cueing him to head out the large double doors.

"What is it?" Eloquine asked. "Is something wrong?"

"No, it's just... Haydn... He has strange things in his castle. It seems he is a lot more apt at simple Earthen science than he gets credit for."

"Oh, no... He gets plenty of credit," she mumbled, her eyes telling Aiella there was still plenty she did not know.

"I know that we talked about him learning Earthen science when his virus became contagious, but I think there is more disease, or magic, or whatever..." Aiella added near-inaudibly, forcing a deep breath to continue on. This had been eating her up all night. "He has a room in his fortress with a label, "For Aiella's execution," and it is filled with a bunch of strange potions or plasma-type material. He has my blood now, and I fear he is mutating ceremotosis."

Eloquine pursed her lips. "We believe that is how he managed to kill some of our ranks fifteen or so years ago. Though it seemed improbable at the time, maybe... maybe we have not minded his abilities enough. Magic and science working together." She shook her head, sighing as she turned around. "That could be catastrophic," she finished.

"It already has been," Aiella told her. "But I think... This may sound crazy, mind you. But I think that he used me to make the ceremotosis progress faster. If I can harness the abilities of the wind, and he has fire..."

"Wind fuels fire," Eloquine finished her thought process.

"Precisely," Aiella confirmed. "I think that's what he did to Frank. But what's terrifying is how quickly he was able to execute that."

"Well, fortunately he is likely gone now. I didn't want to say anything to Lachlan, since Zale was with Haydn. But we have seen no sign of either of them."

Relief set over Aiella in a giant wave before the unpleasant sorrow hit, as well. *Zale.*

"Are you sure?" She asked.

"Not entirely, but pretty positive. We have ranks on the ground there now, searching the area. So far it has, again, been uneventful." When Aiella was speechless, Eloquine added, "Zale could have made it out untraced. He broke off his communication with us a few months ago, fearing Haydn suspected him. We only see Haydn's actions since he's a Guardian. It's like having an invisible aura around you that we can always see. As long as you are above ground."

Aiella nodded her understanding, thanking her for her time. Within seconds, Eloquine disappeared through the door, shutting it softly behind her. Aiella was alone with her thoughts yet again.

Chapter 29

"This is stunning," Aiella commended, a smile flooding her face as she stared ahead at the setup Eloquine had put together for Frank's service. She had spent the rest of the day after meeting Lachlan sobbing in mourning, and she was ready now to remember their time together in peace. To remember her time on Earth, which had abruptly ended. This was a perfect way to do so.

"*You* are stunning," Eloquine complimented. It seemed only right that Aiella wear the sparkling gown that once belonged to her mom, only that wasn't the only adjustment she had made to her appearance. Finding the shears in the drawer in the kitchen, her hair was now healthier and bouncier than ever, the soft ringlets falling just above her shoulders in the front, and just below them in the back. She found a pearly barrette, as the package said, and clipped it to one side of her head, pulling a few curls back with it. It reminded her of what she had looked like when she was younger in the photo with her mother. A dark red coating her lips reflected how much she had grown, and the gown hugged her in all the right places. She could imagine embracing the role of Guardian if this was how she felt every day. It was mesmerizing, and completely confidence boosting.

They had ridden the monorail out of the inner boundaries of the city and into that of the region of Terra. Stepping out into a dense forest, Aiella felt more at home than ever. *Frank would love this,* was her first thought. The midnight blue dress trailed behind her as she walked, light glitter on it twinkling as much as the stars in a night sky. Delicate topaz were clipped onto her ears. The contrast was stunning against her auburn ringlets, now smooth and tamed. It was still bright out, though the time of the Moon's cycle they were in meant a spectacular view for them. The sun was visible on one side of the horizon, with the largely impressive moon, its craters distinguishable from this close, on the other. The tall trees curtained them in some spots almost enough to convince onlookers it was a magical night.

Small, lit up creatures that reminded Aiella of a mix of fireflies and fairies from old tales were scattered up in the branches, a faint humming coming from them in a language she didn't understand. Moss was covering the trunks, but in shades of blue alongside the green, with beautiful golden flowers popping out of them in random places. Once she arrived, she was left in solitude, aside from the stunning creatures high up in the trees. A breeze surrounded her, swirling about as she shut her eyes and concentrated on all the amazing memories she had of her dad. Memories she would cherish forever.

One in particular came to mind. It was only a couple of weeks ago. Aiella had walked to the kitchen, her feet heavier than usual since she knew she was leaving the next day - not knowing when she would return. The reality of everything she had discovered not twenty-four hours later, which had changed all of their lives forever, gave her chills. Thinking back, she always knew Frank knew what she was planning. He was leaning forward over one of the counters, twirling a piece of bark between his fingers.

"Anything else you would like to discuss before heading out to scavenge tomorrow?" He had asked her. She shook her head, Frank giving out a low chuckle.

"Just remember, dear Ella, our happiness is the only thing we are fully in control of." He had walked over to her, given her a hug, and whispered, "I'm so proud of you." Then he kissed her on the forehead and walked out of the room back to bed.

Aiella kept her eyes squeezed shut, willing the memory to not fade. She could feel his presence still there, encouraging her, even after her fatal mistake. She heard a snap, the wind around her picking up turbulence in the circle it was enraged in. Opening her eyes, she saw him. *Frank.*

He was there, right in front of her! Or at least a statue of him was. The wind and earth flourishing with force had formed a beautiful piece of scenery before her. Frank stood suspended within dirt and air in the casual stance against a counter, a smile creasing his eyes. Aiella walked towards it, her hand extended. As quickly as it had formed, it disappeared.

"You broke your concentration," she heard Eloquine's voice to the left of her. That explained the snapping sound. "That was beautiful."

"I did that?" She asked, stunned that she could create such art.

"Mmhm. It will be interesting to see what other abilities you uncover soon." Aiella stood flabbergasted, staring at the spot the figure of Frank had just been. It was the first time she had considered her abilities to be so akin to *magic*. Pure, innocent, stunning magic. The first time her abilities had created something delicate and beautiful, instead of filling the area with destruction. It was breathtaking. Exhilarating.

"Come now," Eloquine said. "I think tomorrow is a perfect day to begin training."

Aiella nodded, taking one last look at the fantastical scene behind her, her fingertips buzzing, her soul ablaze. As she boarded the monorail with the vice chairwoman to head back home, all she could pick up from Eloquine was *hope*.

About the Author

 Breanna Petsch is a writer of children's literature ranging from picture books to young adult. Her passion for storytelling began at an early age, so writing for the growing generations makes sense! She lives a simple life filled with love and creativity in the Inland Northwest, enjoying hiking, reading, living room dance parties, and having tea parties with her husband and kids. Her ideal retreat is curled up in a hammock by a lake with a huge cup of tea in hand. As she continues to explore the possibilities of future narratives, her biggest goal will always be to inspire young readers for years to come.

Acknowledgements

Writing a book is much more of a cooperative project than I think most realize. You need a love of reading, and for this, I give the first thanks to my mom. Without you, I never would have dreamed as a little girl that I could be publishing stories for others to escape reality in. Thank you for helping me find that love from such a young age.

Next, the words themselves need an extra pair of eyes to reach their full potential. The more the merrier! I can't thank every Beta and ARC reader enough for willingly giving my debut a chance before it hit the shelves. To all the people who read my book while it was still on Vella: that includes you! Thank you from the bottom of my heart, your support from the beginning means the world to me. To my editor, Natalia Leigh from Enchanted Ink Publishing, you helped Aiella reach a point I never imagined. Without you, this book would not be what it is and I am forever grateful for your insight!

Thirdly, it takes a lot of courage to put your heart on the page and then release it. Courage that I didn't necessarily have to start. I have to give a special thank you to my sister for pushing me to just go for it, always showing unwavering support, and to my best friend for constantly being my hype girl. Alongside my amazing in-laws, you all were and continue to be my biggest, loudest fans as I embarked on this journey and I love you so much!

Last, but certainly not least, there is no way I could have made this book happen without the love and support of my amazing children and husband. To my three sweet babies, I hope this journey can always serve as a reminder to push through to accomplish your goals, no matter how insurmountable they feel. To my husband, Zach, THANK YOU! We are a team in everything we do in life, and this book is no exception. All the late nights talking about edits and scene changes and publishing plans inbetween all the spit up, neverending diaper changes, and many wrenches Life wanted to throw our way led to this outcome. We've come a long way since walking alongside the road after a high school football game, just talking about all our goals, big and small. Building a life with you and our kids will always be the real dream come true, but this certainly is tasty icing on top of the cake. Thank you for helping me every step of the way to get here. I love you forever.